Anonymous

Hindrances to the Work of the Church in the World: A Series of Sermons

Anatiposi

Anonymous

Hindrances to the Work of the Church in the World: A Series of Sermons

Reprint of the original, first published in 1872.

1st Edition 2023 | ISBN: 978-3-38212-783-1

Anatiposi Verlag is an imprint of Outlook Verlagsgesellschaft mbH.

Verlag (Publisher): Outlook Verlag GmbH, Zeilweg 44, 60439 Frankfurt, Deutschland
Vertretungsberechtigt (Authorized to represent): E. Roepke, Zeilweg 44, 60439 Frankfurt, Deutschland
Druck (Print): Books on Demand GmbH, In de Tarpen 42, 22848 Norderstedt, Deutschland

HINDRANCES TO THE WORK

OF THE

CHURCH IN THE WORLD:

A Series of Sermons,

BY

THE LORD BISHOP OF BATH AND WELLS,
PROFESSOR PLUMPTRE,
CANON WALSHAM HOW,
PREBENDARY ERSKINE CLARKE,
ARCHDEACON SANDFORD,
PREBENDARY HARRIS,
PREBENDARY W. R. CLARK,
PREBENDARY SADLER.

LONDON:
WILLIAM WELLS GARDNER,
2, PATERNOSTER BUILDINGS.

PREFATORY NOTE.

THE occasion on which the following Sermons were preached was the virtual completion of the Renovation of the Church, and particularly of the Chancel, of S. Mary Magdalene, Taunton.

The Sermons are themselves on subjects of such vast importance that it was thought that the deep interest which they excited when they were preached might beneficially be extended beyond our own Parish. I have to thank the Preachers for having added to the first great kindness of preaching their Sermons the additional favour of allowing and superintending their publication.

Of three sermons, which were preached extemporaneously, I have not been able to obtain copies or reports. My best thanks are due to Prebendary Harris and Professor Plumptre for their kindness in supplying the two sermons on *Worldliness* and *Sloth*. I added one of my own, on *Lukewarmness*, to fill up the remaining gap. May God grant of His mercy and grace that the words now sent forth to the Church in the World may help in the removal of some of those many hindrances which impede its work!

W. R. CLARK.

Taunton, Lent, 1872.

CONTENTS:

I.

THE WORK OF THE CHURCH IN THE WORLD,

BY THE

RIGHT HON. AND RIGHT REV. THE LORD BISHOP OF

BATH AND WELLS.

The Work of the Church in the World.

MATT. xvi., 18.

"Upon this Rock will I build My Church."

I SEE before me some hundreds of people—men, women and children. They are of various ages, of various conditions of life, of every station, of every variety of intellectual attainment, pursuing different callings in life, as different in character as they are in dress—in short, high, low, rich, poor, learned, simple. But, whatever diversities may separate one from another, they all are come here in one and the same character, on one and the same footing, by one and the same right and title: they are all members of the Church of God. If we extend our views beyond this Church, and embrace all England, we shall still find that with all the manifold varieties of social position to be found in town and country, and all the divergences caused by different pursuits, there is still the same bond of union and identity, *The Church of God.* Let people be never so different in other respects, they may be one in this, that they are fellow-members of the Church of God.

But we may extend our view far beyond the limits of our native land. If we do so, we shall of course encounter far greater diversities in human nature. We shall come across red men, and yellow men, and black men, and white men, savages and civilised—men speaking divers languages, and not understanding one another's speech. We shall find the most diverse social and political conditions; but we shall also find interpenetrating all these diversities, and binding in one men otherwise most divided, that very same bond which binds us into one body here in Taunton, the bond of fellowship in Christ's Holy Catholic Church. In other words, we find, on examination of the circumstances of the inhabitants of this world, that there is an institution called The Church; that it is co-extensive with the world; that it embraces all nations within its walls; that it imposes identical laws, confers identical privileges, and bestows identical possessions upon them all—yes, upon Englishmen, Hindoos, Hottentots, New Zealanders, Red Indians, and Chinese alike!

But if we enquire further into the origin of this Church, we have to track her way backward through nearly eighteen and a half centuries. It is as if we were tracking some mighty river upwards to its source. As we ascend through centuries past we find the area of the Church on earth gradually narrowing and diminishing, till at length we find it within the four walls of an upper chamber at Jerusalem; or, earlier still, till we come on the Divine presence of Jesus Christ of Nazareth, and hear Him saying to the twelve Apostles, "Upon this Rock I will build My Church." We have now reached the fountain-head of that stream which has gone forth to water the whole earth; or, to pursue the metaphor used by our Lord, we have reached the foundation of the great building. We find that this mighty institution, whose influence embraces all nations, and comprises all ranks in each nation, was founded by the Son of God incarnate, that it is animated by His Spirit, that He is its Living Head, that every part of it is upheld and informed and guided by Him, that this Church is His mystical Body, and that the steps to the formation of this Body were the incarnation of the Word—the birth into this world of the everlasting Son, the human life on earth of Jesus Christ, His cross and passion, His burial and descent into Hell, His glorious resurrection from the dead, and His ascension to the right hand of God in glory. Well, then, what is the work which the Church, thus founded and thus extended, has to perform in the world?

In order to understand and appreciate this work aright we must necessarily first understand the condition of the world itself. Because the Church's work is relative—relative to man's wants, and to man's moral state. The *restoration* of a building implies the knowledge of the architect's original design, and of the subsequent deviations from it. The *healing* of a patient requires the knowledge of his disease, and of the divergence of his organs from health and soundness. So the work of the Church in the world is not what it would have been were the world without sin, but bears a relation to the fallen, corrupt, and sinful state of mankind on earth. In fact, the whole institution of the Church by its Divine Founder is in thought, as in fact, subsequent to, and conditional upon, the fall and ruin of mankind by sin.

Now a hasty glance at the condition of man as he

is seen by the light of history in past ages, and as he is still to be seen by observation at the present day, shows us the evil influence of the fall in these two main points:—

(1) In utter ignorance of the true nature and character of God; and (2) in utter deviation from the rules of righteousness in the dealings of man with man.

I need not stop to illustrate these two heads. The thought of the abominable idolatries and gross superstitions, and polluting services of blood and lust—of the false priesthoods, and idol temples, and blasphemous fables, and childish legends, and debasing conceptions—which everywhere have marked the worship of the gods of the nations, will at once rise up in your minds as proofs of man's ignorance of God. And the past and present condition of the world in respect of wars, strife, oppression, falsehood, and so on, speaks for itself. I may pass on, therefore, to show that the Church's work in the world consists mainly—

I. In bearing witness to the true nature and character of God; and

II. In teaching a true standard of morality between man and man.

I. I conceive that the primary work of the Church on earth is to be a witness for God. God's gift of Revelation to His Church by the Holy Spirit, by the Holy Scriptures, by Apostles and Prophets, is in order to constitute His Church as His witness. Conceive for a moment how supremely important to man, as a reasonable being, the knowledge of God is; what a distortion is caused by false notions of God; what a flood of blessedness comes upon the soul with the knowledge of God! And this knowledge had perished. The world by wisdom knew not God. The world by worldly wisdom never can know God. The Greek with all his acuteness, the Hindoo with all his contemplativeness, the Bhuddist with all his fine-spun sophistries, the modern philosopher with all his scientific accuracy, the Mohammedan with all his dogmatic confidence, have never known God. It is the Church's sublime mission to make Him known—to proclaim His true nature and character; holy, just, and merciful—a Spirit, and yet a Person; a Spirit filling all time and all space with His power and presence; a Person having the closest and most intimate relations to every soul of man. But especially is it the Church's mission to make known the relations of God to man as a sinner. Hence her great theme is redeeming love. She teaches that God is love; but she points her teaching by the love of the crucified Saviour. She teaches God's holiness; but she points her teaching by proclaiming the awful sacrifice of Calvary. She proclaims God's mercy; but she brings home the lesson with irresistible power by testifying to the gift of God's dear Son to be the Saviour of the lost. And in thus bearing witness to God's true character, by proclaiming the great truths of redemption, what a lever does she bring to bear upon the souls of the sinful men whom she teaches! The sinfulness of sin is set forth in the most awful colours; the guilt and danger of sin are shown in all their fulness, and yet a door of escape is set before the sinner with every inducement to him to escape by it. And then how endearing, how inviting, how encouraging is the Church's witness concerning God as the God who hears prayer, who comforts those that are cast down, who does not reject the poor destitute, who heals the broken-hearted, who strengthens the weak, who upholds those that lean upon Him, and saves those who call upon Him! Contrast the experience of Abraham, or David, or St. Paul, in their dealings with God, with the heartless speculations of philosophy, and you will see the immense worth of the Church's witness to the true character of God, and how important a part of her work it is to be God's witness in the world.

I have already pointed out the relation of the great facts of redemption to the Divine nature and character, and it is almost superfluous to add that it is especially by her witness to the death and resurrection of the Lord Jesus Christ, the propitiation for sin, and the Saviour sent by God, that the Church exhibits to the world the true character of God. It is in the face of Jesus Christ that the glory of God shines out with such effulgence.

But no mean part of the Church's testimony is in her offices of public worship. Nothing expresses more clearly and fully the worshipper's conception of God than the kind of worship which is offered to Him. A holy, reasonable, joyful, and spiritual service bears witness to a holy God who is a Spirit and who is love. It is therefore a grave part of the Church's work in the world to keep alive in the world the recollection of God by her devout services, and to take care that those services are such as becomes the God whom we adore. Heathen altars, and heathen sacrifices, and heathen idols, tell an unmistakeable tale of the gods of the heathen. Christian Churches, and Christian worship offered in all faith and love and holy joy, should tell no less distinctly of the holiness and the mercy of the God of our salvation.

As regards God, then, the Church is performing her work in the world aright, when with all her might, by every instrument she possesses—with her voice in preaching, praying, singing; by her action in sacraments, rites, ceremonies, ordinances; by her own holy joy in God's service, and her devout reverence in her ministrations,—she is testifying aloud to the grace and goodness of Almighty God, even as the holy ones in Heaven do who cease not day and night saying, "Holy, Holy, Holy, Lord God Almighty, which was, and is, and is to come." Nor do I think that any graver charge can be brought against any branch of the Church than that by her ordinances of worship she has obscured the true character of God, and borne false witness before the world concerning His nature and attributes, and His kingdom of grace and glory.

II. The other branch of the Church's work is the teaching a true standard of morality between man and man. And this is a work only second to her witness for God. Nothing else can for a moment compare with it in dignity and in importance. Think of all the material improvements that can be effected in man's social condition: unhealthy marshes drained and turned into fruitful fields; waste lands cultivated and teeming with corn and vines, and gardens, and pleasant habitations; railways opening communication from city to city; electric telegraphs annihilating distance; sanitary reforms producing health and cleanliness; education opening up avenues of knowledge to ten thousands, and so on. Place all these in the scale with a real advance in righteousness, a real approximation to God's law of love to man, a real approximation to the mind and character of the Lord Jesus, and they are comparatively but emptiness and vanity. Material improvements with a low morality—falsehood, licentiousness, selfishness—leave man but a whited sepulchre, fair without, all uncleanness within. They leave an outward show of prosperity, with the canker of death gnawing at the heart within. It is as if one decked a corpse in robes of state and called it life. But restore man's nature to the likeness of God in righteousness and true holiness; reinstate his conscience in its rightful supremacy; bring back right as man's rule of conduct, and pluck up wrong by the roots out of the soil of man's heart, and you have made a contribution to human happiness indeed. It is the Church's work on earth to do this. In the midst of all the crookedness of men's ways she shows the straightness of God's law. By the side of human naughtiness she lifts up the model of Christ's most holy life. In the face of maxims and fashions and customs of man's approval she holds out the inimitable beauty of the precepts of the blessed Gospel. She persuades men to eschew the evil and choose the good—to cast off the old man with his deceitful lusts, and to put on the new man. She handles the besom of purification, and would sweep clean out of the world all the defilements brought in by sin. As far as her influence extends, the night of sin recedes, and the morning of righteousness dawns upon the earth.

There was a time when this blessed work seemed likely to be soon realized—when the multitude of them that believed were of one heart and of one soul, eating their meat with gladness and singleness of heart, praising God, and having favour with all the people; and the Lord added to the Church daily such as should be saved. And had that work gone on as it begun, by this time the whole earth had been full of the knowledge of the Lord; every knee would have learnt to bow at the name of Jesus, and the golden age of universal peace and goodwill amongst men would be gladdening the earth. But, alas! the clear shining of that early morn has been followed by a day of clouds and darkness. The swelling buds have withered before they blossomed; the fruit has been bitten by untimely frosts; disappointment has trodden on the heels of hope. But the Church still stands; yea, and shall stand for ever. "The gates of Hell shall not prevail against her." And her work is still the same. He who built her is the same. His promise is the same. His grace is the same as ever. His purpose is the same. Past failures and shortcomings and mistakes have been ours. Doubtless they have done much mischief, and probably that mischief will not cease at once. The children's teeth will be set on edge by the sour grapes which their fathers had eaten. But taking our stand at the present moment, surrounded by existing circumstances, it becomes us to consider the Church's mission from her Divine Head and Founder, and to set ourselves in good earnest to accomplish her proper work.

And I would remind you, my brethren, that in the Church's common work every individual member has to bear his part. The body is not one member, but many. None can delegate his proper function to another. The Church's work in the world is the work of the whole body. Every part and every joint must supply its due share: every stone in the building has its proper place. I showed you in the opening part of my sermon how the Church comprises all grades, and degrees, and ranks, and conditions of men within her pale. It follows that each and all has his part of the Church's work to do. The vessels of wood and earth have their use in the great house, as well as the vessels of gold and silver. The humblest Christian in this Church can contribute his share to the Church's double work of bearing witness for God in the world, and holding out a standard of true morality between man and man, as truly, and perhaps as effectually, as any bishop or any great layman in Christendom. The united testimony of a large body of poor working men, rising above the temptations and difficulties of their station in life, and dignifying their low estate in the world by the ennobling graces of a true Christian walk before God and man, would have an incalculable effect. Try it.

To conclude, and recapitulate: We have seen that the Church's work in the world is—

I. To bear witness for God *(a)* to His being—that there is a God that judgeth the earth *(b)*, to His true nature and character, as opposed to all the false creeds of heathenism, false Christianity, and philosophy *(c)*; to His grace and love as manifested in the redemption of the world by our Lord Jesus Christ, and that so as to draw men to God through Jesus Christ that they may be saved.

II. To set up a true standard of morals, and the methods by which the Church carries on her work in this world is *(a)* by preaching and teaching *(b)*, by the various ordinances of Divine worship, and *(c)* by the exhibition of true godliness in the lives of her members. These methods are simultaneous, mutually supporting each other, and dependent for their success upon their joint action. The Church's instruments are *(a)* her clergy specially set apart for the work of the ministry *(b)*—every individual member of the Body of Christ, every one in whom is the Spirit of Christ, every one who is risen with Christ, every one who is justified by the faith of Christ, who, each in their proper place and sphere, have the Church's work committed to them by the Great Head Jesus Christ as truly as the clergy have theirs.

And I observe, lastly, that the area within which this work has to be done is the world—this world of God's making, with man upon it. From the hill on which God has built this city—the Church—we, my brethren and fellow-citizens, must take a survey of the habitable globe. We must look near, and we must look far, wherever there are tokens of human habitations, wherever there are men—men of like passions with ourselves, men with souls like our souls, men who are God's creatures as we are God's creatures. As we look we shall see sin, sorrow, death. But we shall remember, God made those souls; they are His in spite of all their sins. Jesus Christ died for those souls. They are His in spite of all their sins. And we must resolve that they shall be won back to God through Jesus Christ, if God permit. Resolving this, we must set the Church's machinery to work in good earnest to win them.

With courage, but with wisdom; with determination, but with meekness; with burning zeal, but with kind forbearance; with utter self-abnegation, with entire simplicity of aim, with our whole strength, with unflagging perseverance, with concentration of purpose, and in entire dependence upon the grace and strength of Jesus Christ, we must pursue the work entrusted to us. The assault must be made on all the strongholds of sin. The vices of the rich, the vices of the poor, the evil fashions of a corrupt world, whether in high life or low life, the false maxims of a worldly morality, the false theology of a spurious philosophy, the false tenets of a corrupt religion, the ignorance and the wickedness of men wherever they are found —against these, I say, and every other form of falsehood and wrong, we must bring the Church's holy warfare to bear. Everywhere we must strive to make known Almighty God, manifested in His only begotten Son, Jesus Christ. Everywhere we must strive to establish Christ's blessed law of truth and purity and love. God grant that in the day when the glorious Church is presented unto Christ in her bridal beauty of spotless holiness it may be found that we in this corner of the earth, in this our generation, have not wasted our opportunities, but that we have done our part, by the grace of God, in forwarding the Church's work in the world, of witnessing for God our Heavenly Father, and teaching all men the right ways of Jesus our Saviour!

II.

DELAYS AND DIFFICULTIES IN THE CHURCH'S WORK,

BY THE

REV. E. H. PLUMPTRE, M.A.,

PROFESSOR OF DIVINITY IN KING'S COLLEGE, LONDON; PREBENDARY OF S. PAUL'S, AND RECTOR OF PLUCKLEY, KENT.

Delays and Difficulties in the Church's Work.

REV. vi., 10.

"How long, O Lord, holy and true."

THE cry which the seer of Patmos heard, as in these words, from the souls that were beneath the altar, as they waited with patience for the unfolding of God's purposes and the triumph of His saints, is one which has been raised in every tone of sadness, wonder, almost despair, by thousands in every age. Its exceeding bitterness has for the most part been in exact proportion to the intensity of man's belief in the holiness and righteousness of God. The man who passes through life moved only by the lower pleasures and lower pains which he shares with the brute creatures round him — he who fixes on some end in life, power, wealth, honour, and pursues it with a restless egotism—he who has attained to the serener temper which takes men and things as they are, and seeks to make the best of them—these may have other sorrows, other struggles; but that of this perplexity and expectancy, the "hope deferred" that "maketh the heart sick," is not of them. It is precisely because they are "men of desires," craving for the kingdom of Heaven, longing for a world in order, that the disorders and confusions, in the midst of which they live, weigh on the servants of God with so intolerable a burden, that the delays and difficulties in working out what they are sure is the Divine purpose for themselves and for mankind lead to such passionate complaints. That feeling is recognised, expressed, met as far as it can be met, in the Book which is at once so intensely human and so essentially divine. Hints and suggestions are thrown out that the mystery of permitted evil, and of good thwarted or delayed, lies altogether behind the veil, beyond the ken even of angelic vision, or prophet's inspiration, or the knowledge of the spirits of the just in the Paradise of God. It is not from the prophet's lips, in that wondrous vision of Zechariah's, that the cry "How long?" proceeds, but from those of "The Angel of the Lord." (Zech. i., 12.) It is not from those who are fighting the battle and falling in the breach that it is heard to rise in the Apocalypse, but from the "souls beneath the altar that were slain for the Word of God, and for the testimony which they held," who were clothed already in the white robes of victory. (Rev. vi., 11.) And in each case words were spoken in reply, which, if they did not solve the problem, or disclose that which can be known only to Him who sees the end from the beginning, were at least enough to strengthen and sustain the doubting heart and give it courage to endure. The prophet heard, as from the lips of the Lord of Hosts himself, the "good and comfortable words" which assured him, as he brooded over the desolation of the Holy City, that the Lord would yet "comfort Zion," and would yet "choose Jerusalem." (Zech. i., 13, 17.) The Apostle heard that it was said to the souls which raised that exceeding bitter cry that they should "rest yet a little season" in the peace and rest of God, which He gives to His chosen ones, till the gathering of the Martyrs' army had been completed and the appointed time had come.

Such thoughts as these may help, in some measure, to counterbalance the sense of failure and disappointment which comes over us as we survey the history of the world,—yet more, because we look to it as called into being to redress, at least, some of the world's disorders,—as we trace the history of the Church. So many high energies wasted and misapplied; so many noble institutions decaying and waxing old, losing their life and becoming fruitful only in corruption, prejudices, misunderstandings; the bitterness of party dividing those who ought to be ot one heart and one soul in the fellowship of God's saints; epochs when there seemed to be a brighter future dawning on the destinies of mankind, and men heard, as on the mountain heights, the cry of those who published glad tidings of salvation, passing away and leaving the old evils of the world unredressed;—generation after generation forced to utter the same wail of lamentation, "The harvest is over, the summer is ended, and we are not saved;"—all this is dark and depressing enough. The same sentence of incompleteness seems to rest alike upon the dreams of those who have lived in visions of human progress and perfectibility resting on political or social changes, and on those who looked to some renewal or revival of the Pentecostal gifts and the strength that comes from God. If we point to the great revolution which closed the last century, and of which we are yet feeling the terrible vibrations, as an example of the one, we must remember that the Reformation was hailed with not less ardent hopes, and has met with no less disastrous a frustration—that the lesser religious movements in the history of our own and other churches, which to those who started or shared in them seemed to be as the coming of God's kingdom, may be reckoned by the score. Do not our own experience, the memories of the last few years, the history of the life and work of each one of us, in town or village, in church or school, bring back to us failures, like in kind, which have wounded us yet more keenly? An impulse has been given to our life, or to that of one whose soul was dear to us as our own, which seemed to promise a great change for good. There was, we hoped, the unfolding of the regenerate life. Old things had passed away, and, behold, all things were becoming new. And then temptations have come, and sin has revived in all its power to deceive and to destroy, and the likeness of the old evil self has re-appeared in all its foulness, and the latter end has been worse than the beginning. Or we have seen the commencement of a like work among those for whose souls we were called to watch. Some new organisation, some mission or revival, some guild or association, gave promise of a better future for our parish. There was a stirring among the dry bones, as if the breath of the Spirit of the Lord was bringing them together and infusing life, not into dead forms only, but into hearts and souls that were dried up and withered, and we trusted that they would rise up "an exceeding great army." Services were better attended, communions more visibly and on a larger scale means of blessing to the faithful, worship more hearty and rejoicing, and then there has come opposition, and irritation, and rebuke and blasphemy from without, or deadness and lukewarmness from within. Delays and difficulties have multiplied around us at every step. We have been tempted to fold our hands in the silent acquiescence of despair, or the cry, "How long, O Lord, how long?" has mingled with our sighs and tears.

Thoughts like these may seem sad and depressing, out of harmony with the temper of Christian hope. But there is, we may be sure, here also, as with all facts which we look steadily in the face, a sweetness that follows on the bitter, lessons of wisdom and of patience not otherwise to be learnt.

1. It is well not to be over sanguine in the expectations with which we start. We must not expect that the world will be converted, or a Church renew its youth like the eagle, in the course of a single generation, or a parish be of one mind in all things, or an individual soul raised to the blessedness of the new life by the power of a single sermon or a week such as that on which we are now entering. Every age of the Church—the first not excepted—has had, as we have seen, its share of such exaggerated hopes. They are, perhaps, almost inseparable from the impulse which leads men to earnest and self-devoted work. Think, for a moment, of that which had floated before the minds of the personal disciples of Our Lord, and of those who immediately succeeded them. The times and the seasons not being revealed to them, they

were left free, in some measure at least, to draw pictures of the future for themselves. And those pictures were, as is obvious, altogether wanting in perspective. They were already, they thought, in the last days. The end was near at hand, the Judge was standing at the door. They saw, or thought they saw, the Gospel already preached to every nation under Heaven; its heralds already gone out into all lands, and their voice unto the ends of the world. Events of colossal greatness in God's spiritual order were to crowd upon each other in rapid succession. The rejection of Israel that the Gentiles might be received; the apostasy that was to end in the revelation of the Man of Sin; the restoration of Israel as life from the dead—all these entered into their anticipations of what they, or those who were growing up around them, might live to witness. And then there came, when the years passed on and the hopes remained unfulfilled, and heresies and divisions multiplied around and within the Church, the inevitable reaction. Scoffers took up their taunting proverb and asked, "Where, then, is the promise of His coming?" The hearts of the righteous were made sad as they entered on a state of things so different from all they had anticipated. First to one and then to another glimpses were given as to the possible postponement of the closing scene of the world's great drama. At last the truth was proclaimed which in its exceeding breadth covers these and all like cases—"One day is with the Lord as a thousand years, and a thousand years as one day." (2 Peter iii., 8.) Men, even Apostles, are impatient and for precipitating things, asking, "Wilt thou at this time?" (Acts i., 6.) "How long, O Lord, holy and true?" but He, the Author of Nature, the Lord and King of that which, though supernatural is yet subject to the law of the same eternal will, appears to be "deliberate in all His operations, accomplishing His ends by slow, successive steps." *

The gain of receiving, acting on, living in that truth is clearly immense. If we do not expect success rapid, unbroken, wide-spreading, as the result of our labours, we shall not be disappointed and downhearted when we meet with failure. If we lose something of the brightness and joy of the hopes that lead men on, we escape at least the heart-sickness of hope deferred. We are led to make, not success, but duty, the motive and measure of our work. In proportion as we estimate rightly the instability of the praise and sympathy which are at first so pleasant, and seem to promise so rapid a fulfilment to our highest hopes, it becomes a very small thing to us to be judged of man's judgment; and it becomes more and more the law of our nature to work ever as in the Great Task-Master's eye, and to remember that He that judgeth us is the Lord. The old chivalrous watchword of *Fais ton devoir, avvienne que pourra* may well be emblazoned on the shields and engraved on the hearts of the soldiers of the cross. We can learn no higher lesson than that which has been taught us by a poet of our own, that—

> Because right is right, to follow right
> Is wisdom, in the scorn of consequence.

2. But there is a worse evil even than that of these exaggerated and feverish hopes, leading to more

* Butler's Analogy, part ii., cap 4, *ad fin.*

utter unreality, against which also we should guard. Men *affect* to have the hopes—make-believe, sometimes to others, sometimes even to themselves—that they do not see the delays and difficulties which a clearer vision discerns to be inevitable. We have all of us listened to, many of us have been tempted to use, language of this nature. Statesmen and orators feed the imagination of the fierce democracy which they seek to wield at will with prognostications of a political millennium, the halcyon days of peace and plenty, Astrea upon earth again, and the golden age returned. The platform rhetoric of Church Congresses, and Social Science reformers, and missionary meetings, reverberates with platitudes of this kind—hollow, windy, unsubstantial, which those who utter them, and those who hear, alike know to be insincere. The reunion of Christendom, the healing of the schisms that divide our own portion of it, the extinction of pauperism, ignorance, crime, are spoken of as if the harvest was already ripe, waiting only to be gathered in. We smile at the fault when it appears in yet greater and more morbid forms in nations of warmer temperament and less restrained language than ourselves; but there, for the most part, (take, for example, the manifestoes of French Communists and Italian Revolutionists,) men themselves believe, even with a strong delusion, in the dreams with which they deceive others. The insincerity is greater in us who, with our cooler, more phlegmatic nature, see more clearly how far the performance will fall short of the glory of the promise.

3. Soberness, then, and reticence—the self-restraint in thought and speech which is the temper of the wise of heart—are the lessons which we have to learn

as we look out upon the work which we have to do and the impediments which we are sure to meet with. But this is not all. We need something more, and, thank God, something more has been given us, than the philosophic indifference which in life accepts the inevitable as in speculation it learns to keep within the limits of the knowable,—something more even than the more heroic temper of the Stoic, who, even though the gods seemed on the side of the oppressor, was content to take his part with the oppressed. A new hope, deeper, brighter, entering into that within the veil, takes the place of the hopes, light-minded fickle and fantastic, which have become a bye-word of reproach. It is given to us to live by faith, not by sight, to cherish the belief that we are fellow-workers with God, and that His righteous purposes of justice or of love will, sooner or later, assuredly fulfil themselves. We may well be content with the thought that we are labourers in His vineyard, servants of whom the Great Master is not unmindful; called at the third, or sixth, or ninth hour; sent to occupy till He come with our ten talents, or five, or one; casting the seed of the Word of Life on the highway, or the rock, or among thorns, or on the good ground; stewards of the mysteries of God, of whom it is required that they should be found faithful. We should live in the belief that He has given us our work, is with us as we labour; gives us the strength needed for our day; will with temptations make a way to escape. Every true word spoken, every good deed done, every victory over one's self, does something—how little or how much we know not—to the fulfilment of His purpose and the consummation of His kingdom. A law fulfilling itself in the midst of apparent anomalies: the maintenance of stability in the strife of seemingly conflicting forces; apparent waste and failure, while yet a clearer vision discerns a conservation of force, and rejects the thought that failure or waste is possible; the evolution of higher forms of life from lower, with intervals which seem to interrupt the succession, with a return to the inferior type,—this, which science has learnt to recognise in the material world, has its counterpart, more or less distinctly visible to the illumined vision, in God's spiritual kingdom. And He, in His Word, has taught us some, at least, of the laws by which this end is attained. "Herein is this saying true, one soweth and another reapeth." (John iv., 37.) No man knows on earth the extent of the work which he does on earth whether for good or evil. If it is sometimes given to those who go on their way weeping and bearing precious seed to come again with joy and bring their sheaves with them, (Psalm cxxvi., 6,) it is yet true that many men labour only that others may enter into their labours, and see not in what way or to what extent they have forwarded the cause for which they have been content to labour and to die. Workers in building up the Church of God, the Temple not made with hands, with the living stones, which are the elect of God, they have not known the plans of the Divine Architect, nor even as a wise master-builder appreciated its symmetry and beauty; but if they have been faithful in the work assigned them, faithful even in a very little, they shall in no wise lose their reward. Even mistakes and failures are pardoned where there is the willing heart that labours in its love of Christ. Even though the wood, hay, stubble may be consumed in the fire which tries every man's work of what sort it is, the man himself, if he has built on the one foundation, shall be saved so as by fire.

Thus then it stands. The action of many forces working in many different ways, rather than immediate and short-lived success—progress by antagonism, the conflict of different tendencies bringing out the truth which is in each, and revealing the falsehood which was mingled with it; change rather than sameness, and unity as distinct from uniformity;—this is the law of God's kingdom, and the thought that it is so will help us to view with calmness what might otherwise oppress us with despondency, and to face the difficulties which beset us, and the delays which are interposed between our hopes and their fulfilment. We must be content to see that law of change and decay written, now as in past ages, on much that is very precious to us—on institutions, customs, forms of worship, aspects of the truth, which have seemed to us inseparably associated with the Eternal Truth itself. So it has been always, and so it will be to the end. The ideal of the Patriarchs was not that of those who lived under the law. That which the Prophets saw in vision had a new glory of its own. The Apostolic age, the Church of the fourth century, Western Christendom in its mediæval period, the Reformed Churches in our own and other lands, the founders of Orders and of Missions, the great teachers and preachers of their time, have all had, each of them, their own standards of excellence, their own hopes, their own ideals. We look back and see that it would not have been well for the Church or for mankind if any one of them had become dominant. We can see that each has left its mark, for good as well as evil—yes, for good more than evil—on the history of the world; and if we read the past so that it becomes to us, not as an old almanack, but a prophecy of the future, we may well believe and even hope that it will be so with much that we now wrangle and debate about—with questions as to words and names, and vestments and positions, the relations between science and religion, between Church and State. To work calmly, patiently, steadfastly, at the special tasks which God has given us to do—to do with our might whatever our hand findeth to do—to work without passion and without panic—to remember that the truth of God has issued victorious out of more terrible conflicts than any that now await it—this will be at once our wisdom and our blessedness. If we sow without reaping, there is also for us the assurance that he that soweth and he that reapeth shall rejoice together. If things that seemed sacred and venerable are decaying and waxing old, and ready to vanish away—if there are signs of the removal of the things that are shaken, it is only that the things which cannot be shaken may remain. So the world's great drama passes through its successive stages to its appointed end, and our incompleteness works out God's completeness, and our restlessness is hushed and quieted in His rest; so—

> "God fulfils Himself in many ways,
> Lest one good custom should corrupt the world."

In His light we shall see light, though the mist and darkness now lie thick around us. What we need is enough light to see our path, though it were but a single step before us,—to lead us, with its kindly radiance, through the encircling gloom; and that light is given to us, even as it is given to every man that cometh into the world—given to us in yet greater clearness because we walk in His light who is the brightness of His Father's glory and the express image of His person. Only while we have the light let us walk in the light, and be as children of the light; for if we walk in self-chosen darkness, the darkness which we love rather than light because our deeds are evil—we shall stumble; and on all of us in a few years the night cometh—the night of death,—when no man can work.

III.

SPIRITUAL FEVER,

BY THE

REV. W. WALSHAM HOW, M.A.,

HON. CANON OF S. ASAPH, RECTOR OF WHITTINGTON, SALOP,

AND RURAL DEAN.

Spiritual Fever.

S. John iv., 52.

"Yesterday at the seventh hour the fever left him."

It must be a familiar thought to all of you that the various diseases of the body are types and likenesses of corresponding diseases of the soul, and that our Lord's many miracles of healing are also parables, setting Him forth to us as the Great Healer of all spiritual maladies. Thus that terrible scourge of the Eastern nations—leprosy, spreading, as it did, over the whole frame, poisoning the springs of life, and eating into every vital power,—is, alas! too faithful a likeness of the utter depravity of man's fallen nature, when his terrible inheritance of sin is left to bring forth its natural fruit, unchecked by Divine grace. So, too, in the blind, and the deaf, and the dumb; we see ever pictures of those who, having eyes, will not see the things of God; who are spiritually deaf, so that they listen not to the counsels of His will; and spiritually dumb, so that they have no voice of inward prayer, no tongue to set forth the praises of their Creator and their Redeemer. Again, the palsied frame may very fitly set forth to us the soul lying in the helpless paralysis of apathy, and coldness, and indifference. Of this I propose to speak to you tomorrow. While the fever of the body may well picture to us the more active and violent forms of sin, those which belong to the passions, and which are not so much sins forming a part of the general character and weaving themselves into the whole texture of the soul, as sins which appear as occasional inroads into the ordinary tenor of the life—outbreaks more or less frequent of a hidden fire, which smoulders within, and reveals itself only when some new fuel is cast upon it. This class of sins, which I have called "Spiritual Fever," will be my subject to-night.

But, first, let me try to picture the scene, from the history of which I have taken my text. Our Lord is again at Cana in Galilee, where he had performed His first miracle—that, namely, of changing water into wine. A certain "nobleman" came to Him. Literally it is a *royal* personage, one closely connected in some way with the court, such as was Chuza, Herod's steward. He is a great man; yet he travels all the way from Capernaum, where his home is, to Cana, that he may meet Jesus, of whose visit he has heard, and make his humble request. He is in great trouble, for his son is at the point of death, dying of a fever. And how terrible to be away from that bedside all those long hours! How the picture of his child, as he has left him in his deadly peril, must haunt him all the way! Those glazed, wandering eyes: those sunken, burning cheeks: those dry, parched, blackened lips: that quick, panting, gasping breath: how the scene must perpetually stand before him! How it must spur and goad him on! And so, when Jesus begins to moralise about it, as it would seem to him, and says, "Except ye see signs and wonders ye will not believe," the poor agonised father exclaims, with a pardonable impatience, "Sir, come down ere my child die." Yes, it is his only chance. If only he may be in time! If only he can persuade this great Healer to come at once, ere his child die! But there is no need for Him to come. He can heal near or far off. He can take Peter's wife's mother by the hand and raise her up, or speak a single word miles away, and the fever is stayed. Even as the winds and the waves obeyed His "Peace, be still," so the raging fever owns His sway. It is over. The eye rests calmly; the parched, burning skin is soft and cool again; the panting breath comes gently and peacefully! How startling the change to the watchers by that suffering bed, who know not the secret of the cure! Here we behold Jesus the healer of the fever of the body. We will now think of Him as the healer of the fever of the soul.

This spiritual fever is chiefly found in characters of some force and strength. It besets a very opposite class of persons to those I shall speak of to-morrow. *They*, the victims of spiritual palsy, are lying in the helpless apathy of perpetual sins of omission; *these*, the fever patients, are struggling under the desperate tyranny of masterful sins of commission. They are strong, eager, vehement, impetuous natures who suffer most from spiritual fever. Well, let them not complain. They may have a harder struggle; yet perchance there is in store for them a nobler victory. Great saints have often been, like the great St. Augustine, men of strong, wilful passions. I think St. Peter and St. Paul were men who in their youth were more likely to have had to do battle with the assaults of hot passions than with the temptation to selfish, apathetic indolence. In all forcible characters there must be a great and fierce battle with the powers of evil. In one way the parallel between our Lord's bodily healings and His spiritual healings does not hold good. The fever of the soul is not banished in a moment. Even when the patient is recovering, it is as with an intermittent fever. The complaint is ever renewing itself. It breaks out again and again. And yet—oh! believe it, for it is true—Jesus *will* at length give you the victory; He *will* speak the word of healing to your soul. He *can*, and He *will*. Though the battle be long, though the fever be oftentimes renewed, though you may even have to suffer from outbreaks of your besetting sin to the very end, yet victory is sure. Sooner or later it will come. The mighty Healer has not lost His power. I have told you the cure will not be sudden. I also tell you it may not be wholly wrought out in you on this side of the grave. It is not he who has won an old victory who is crowned, but he who is found fighting faithfully to the end. But this I do promise you, that, just as a constitution is strengthened by due dieting and proper medicines and tonics to throw off attacks of fever which might otherwise have been fatal, so will your souls, strengthened and disciplined by the wholesome medicines of God's Word and nourished by the Bread of Life, be enabled better and better, as you go on, to resist the attacks of spiritual fever, and to triumph over the violence of your besetting sins.

To deal with this fever of the soul, let us try to understand the real character of the disease. Where is its seat in our nature? What is it that really makes it dangerous? How shall we know whether we are getting better or worse? Now it is of first importance to understand that all sin has its true seat in the *will*. The consent of the will is necessary to constitute any action either good or bad. Without the action of the will there is no moral character in anything we do. Therefore in this matter of spiritual fever we must look to the will, if we would either understand its sinfulness or apply any availing remedy.

If the consent of the will is needful to give to an action its character for good or evil, plainly the first thing to do, when the assault of sin comes, is, to *refuse the consent of the will*. It is possible you may yet be a victim to the fever—that in spite of your resolution your will may be overcome, and you may be hurried into your old besetting sins. But you have gained something—at least you have made a beginning—if you can turn sins of will into sins of weakness.

The next step is so to strengthen the will as to make it able to withstand even sins of weakness. It must become *strong to resist*. Before, it yielded, as it were, under protest; now, it must refuse to yield at all. And every victory will make this easier. Every time the fire of temptation is crushed down under the heel of a resolute will by the grace of God, it will be weakened for the next outbreak.

And then there is a third stage of advance, but not given to all. When you have first turned the sins of will into sins of weakness, and have then strengthened your will to refuse to yield to sins of weakness, go on, if God give you strength, to *seek the opposite grace* to the sin which has been once your snare. This is hard, but not too hard for the power of God. If you have been violent and rough of temper, strive to win the grace of meekness. If you have given way to passionate lusts, strive to win the grace of purity. Such is the true course of the recovery. Although the fever spread through every part and every sense, so that the whole head is sick and the whole heart faint—so that from the sole of the foot to the crown of the head there is no soundness—yet the treatment must be in the will. We are never healed apart from our wills—that is, apart from ourselves. Christ conquers for us; but at the same time He conquers *in* us and *through* us. He, as it were, enlists us to fight against ourselves. He makes us, in a sense, our own physicians.

But to work out the cure as I have described it we have sore need of two things—watchfulness and prayer. Take the case of one in whom the fever of sin burns—perhaps not at this moment, but from time to time. He asks, "How shall I escape from this miserable disease of my soul?" His sin troubles him in his calmer moments. He looks back upon his outbreaks of passion—violent tempers—harsh, bitter, or blasphemous words — intemperance in drink — unbridled thoughts—or the like. They trouble him sorely. He is told to resist and to subdue them. But he knows not how. What shall we tell him? How shall we treat the case?

1. He must *watch*. He must learn to know the first signs of an approaching attack. He must understand the first faint symptoms of the malady. He must note what outward things, or persons, or circumstances, seem to give rise to it; and he must guard against these. Many a time a medicine taken

at the first sign of approaching sickness has prevented it altogether, when at a later stage it would have been wholly useless.

2. He must *pray*. He must go to Jesus, and ask Him to help him—ask Him to turn his will against his besetting sin, that he may fight against it manfully. He must pray. And when I say this, I do not mean only that he must pray at all times: this is needful: but I mean that he must pray when beset with his malady. I know, my brethren, how hard this is. I know how hard it is, when passion is firing the heart, and the flame of evil desire or of unholy temper is kindling within us, to turn and face God. It often seems a wrench too violent to make. God holds out to us the very weapon which alone can save us, and we turn away and will not grasp it. But if we would not perish, the effort *must* be made. Yes, even in the moment of temptation, when the whole soul rebels against the thought of God, we must force ourselves to put up the cry, "Lord save me; I perish!" It is hard to do it; but the Lord is only waiting for the cry, to stretch forth His hand and lift us out of the whelming waters.

And then, lastly, let us know well the difference between temptation and sin—between natural weakness, aye, and weakness brought on by former sins, on the one side, and consent of will on the other. Temptation is not sin; else the Son of God sinned, for He was tempted. Natural weakness, though of the nature of sin, and though it predisposes to sin, is not charged against us as sin so long as it is resisted and fought against. Even weakness brought on by former indulgence—weakness which we owe and can trace to former sin and selfishness—even this will not be imputed to us as present sin, if the soul hate it, and the will withstand. These things are great trouble, great grief, great shame, to the sufferer; but they are not of necessity sin. Nothing is really sin in which the will gives no consent. Nothing past, nothing present, can hurt the soul if the will holds fast by God, who will hold *it* fast. No storm of passion rushing over the soul—no violence of assault, though it shake the soul through and through—no quickening of the soul's pulse to fever quickness—no powerlessness even to get rid of the thought which the soul hates—can hurt the soul, if there be not the least consent of will. But, oh! do not mistake me. Dare we be careless then, and suffer lightly the presence of evil in our souls? Nay, this is itself the consent of will. God forbid that I should even seem to make light of sin. I only want to comfort and help those who are truly striving to be free from sin. I have not the least word of comfort for the willing captive to sin. You find yourselves very weak and helpless. Well, you have brought this on yourselves. All this trouble and difficulty in shaking off the attacks of sin is too faithful a witness to your past sinful compliance. It tells you how much you have to mourn over and confess in former days. If from early youth you had stedfastly set yourself to resist, oh! how easy it would have been by this time! And yet, even now, I say, if Jesus is making your will sound, all will be well. The root is there—in the will. Let that become healthy, and the life and actions must follow in the end. Only seek that Saviour's help more earnestly. Grasp His hand tighter. Cling to the hem of His garment. You shall not die of the fever. You may be very sick, and very miserable.

But, oh! the day is at hand when you shall put off for ever all this remaining corruption—when you shall be delivered indeed from the body of this death. For this body, now so full of evil, supplying now the fuel on which the fire of spiritual fever feeds—this body, so sad an instrument in Satan's hands—this body shall itself be instinct with new life, and the whole man, shaking off and leaving behind all that is gross, earthly, fallen, shall be conformed for ever to the glorious likeness of the sinless One! And when we wake up after that likeness we shall be satisfied.

IV.

SPIRITUAL PARALYSIS,

BY THE

REV. W. WALSHAM HOW, M.A.,

HON. CANON OF S. ASAPH, RECTOR OF WHITTINGTON, SALOP, AND RURAL DEAN.

Spiritual Paralysis.

St. Matt. ix., 6.

"Arise, take up thy bed and go unto thine house."

Palsy, or paralysis, as the word in our Bibles means, is one of the saddest, most helpless, most hopeless, of complaints. We all know, when some friend has (as we say) had a stroke, and lost the use of his limbs; and when, day after day, and then month after month, has passed by without material improvement, how all hope dies out in us. We wait, but for the end. We have ceased to think of a cure. We are only thankful to know that there is little pain and suffering.

This is a picture of a soul in a state of spiritual numbness, and coldness, and deadness. I am to speak to you to-night of this state as a hindrance to the work of the Church in the world; and if the line I take is more personal than the general subject of these sermons might lead you to expect, it is because I am deeply impressed with the conviction that there is no royal road to the conversion of the world, and that the work of the Lord has to be done, not by machinery, not by organisation, not by legislation, (though, indeed, all these have their place and their power,) but by patient dealing with individual souls. My brethren, I know not whether the form of spiritual disease I am to speak of to-night—the soul's deadening paralysis—or that which I spoke of last night—the active fever of passion—is the greater impediment to the advance of holiness. But this I know, that among earnest seekers after God, when they open their heart's troubles to their ministers, few things are more often said than this—"I cannot love God." "I am so cold," they say, "so dead, so unloving! I do want to love God; but it seems as if there were no power in me to stir the stagnant surface of my chill affections or to make their waters flow. Prayer, which ought to be so blessed and joyous a thing, is a task and not a joy: the Bible, which ought to be an absorbing delight, is far less interesting to me than any other book. Even Holy Communions themselves, which I well know ought to fill my whole soul with loving adoration and to bring me to Jesus with the outpouring of tenderest emotions—even these are dull, dry, formal. Jesus seems so far off! I know what I need—His warm, loving, healing touch. But I can't reach out and grasp His hand. I can't even put out my poor palsied hand so far as to touch the hem of His garment. Oh! this dryness of spirit!—this hard, insensate, unloving heart of mine! What shall I do to escape from this terrible paralysis of soul?" So speaks many a poor anxious soul, when something comes which arouses it to a sense of its own state and makes it yearn for release. God sends messengers to it to carry it to Jesus, just as the four kind friends carried the poor paralytic man. Perhaps (oh! blessed if it be so, both for me and for thee!)—perhaps God has sent me this night to some one among you to be a bearer to take you to Jesus. O thou poor paralysed soul! I come to thee to call thee to Him who only can speak the word of healing and set thee free. I come to take thee to thy Saviour, to carry thee to His blessed presence, to bring thee to His holy feet.

Now there is one thing you may say, if you will:—many say it:—"*Let me alone.*" Ah! yes; there is no acute pain which *must* be felt; no burning fever which *must* alarm; no loss of sight or hearing which *must* cry aloud for recovery. It is the very peril of this paralysis that it pains not. "*Let me alone,*" you may say; "I am not so bad as you think; I am not leading a wicked life; I don't feel so dangerously ill. True, I may not be as eager, and earnest, and devout as some; but perhaps that is my nature. I am not one of strong emotions; I am naturally calm and cold. Any how I don't want to be disturbed and made uncomfortable. *Let me alone.*" You have only to go back to the beginning of the chapter from which I have taken my text to see what is the suro result of such an answer as that. At the end of the last chapter we see the whole city of the Gadarenes going out to meet Jesus. And no wonder. For had He not just conferred upon them the most signal mercy? Had He not just delivered them from the awful scourge under which they had so long suffered, healing that dreadful savage demoniac who had been the terror of their neighbourhood? No wonder they all went out to meet Him. Surely it must be to pray Him to come into their city—to tell Him of other sick and suffering ones, and to beseech Him to come and cure them. But can it be true? "When they saw Him"—aye, there is the wonder—"when they *saw* Him"—when they saw that gentle, loving Face, so full of mercy and tenderness,—"when they saw Him, they besought Him to depart out of their coasts." They did not want to be upset and made uncomfortable. Why, He might have said, "Woe unto you, ye Gadarenes," as He said, "Woe unto you, Chorazin and Bethsaida!" They had no wish to have their sins dragged to light. They did very well as they were, and so they said, "Let us alone;" and *He let them alone.* For, if we read straight on, without the break in the chapters, which is in this place somewhat unfortunate, we are told that "they besought Him that He would depart out of their coasts; and He entered into a ship, and passed over, and came into His own city." It is always the law of His blessings. They are for those who ask. They are withheld from those who are content to be without them.

But I think those who would say "Let us alone" will hardly be in this Church to-night. I believe, if I am speaking to any souls lying bound in the chains of spiritual paralysis, they are such as bewail their unhappy state, and long to be set free.

Well, then, let us go to the root of the matter; for, until we can trace out the cause of a disease we are not very likely to find the remedy; and oftentimes the finding of the cause is at the very same time the finding of the remedy.

This paralysis of the soul has many causes. Shall I guess at some? I can but draw my bow at a venture; but God may perchance direct the shaft.

1. Is it wilful sloth and indolence? You know

sloth has been reckoned one of the seven deadly sins. It seems to you, perhaps, a light sin by comparison with many others. Ah! but have you ever thought how much that is amiss in you may be traced to this one root? For instance, how often is sloth the true cause of that prayerlessness against which you were so powerfully warned this morning. It requires exertion and effort to put the soul in the posture of prayer; and sloth is an averseness to all exertion and effort. Perhaps you cannot test sloth better than by your devotions. Are they apt to be short, and weary, and cold, and beset by wandering thoughts? Then you may suspect the presence of sloth in your soul. Nay, I may go to more outward things; for, shame though it be to say it, even our outward attitude and bearing may be a test to us of sloth. Are there none whose prayers are prayed—not, indeed, standing at the corner of the streets, but—*leaning on their beds*? whose morning prayer is a hurried repetition of a scanty form, and whose evening prayer a sleepy attempt to say through the appointed words of devotion?

Do not think outward idleness a necessary sign of sloth. Sloth is often found co-existing with great outward activity. But how can this be? Simply because this outward activity is natural and easy, and needs little or no effort. You see a man always busy, full of energy, and perhaps devoting that energy to good works, and you say, "In that man at least sloth can have no place," and you little suspect perhaps that all the time in that busy, restless, energetic man this deadly sin of sloth may be eating into the very core of his heart, and destroying all his fixedness of will and power of self-sacrifice.

2. Is it possible—I know that it is possible, but is it *true?*—that in your heart there lurks some secret lust, the occasional indulgence of impure thoughts, the scarcely acknowledged love of impure fancies, such as may be cherished by an unchastened, unguarded eye or ear? Oh! these things, beloved brethren, more than aught else, are destructive of spiritual life, and healthfulness, and activity. You wonder at your soul's deadness to heavenly things. Can it be that this worm is in the bud, eating out its life and fair beauty? It is hard to speak of these things to a mixed congregation; yet I dare not be silent. I should not be faithful if I were silent, when I am trying to point out to you the causes of spiritual paralysis. It is no use beating about the bush. It is no use mincing matters, when those matters are matters of life and death. I will tell you one thing, as a sample of the sort of evil I am speaking of. If a young man takes pleasure in reading such reading as the reports of divorce cases in the newspapers, he must not be surprised if he falls into spiritual paralysis. He is taking the poison into his system which will most surely produce the disease.

3. Is it the case that you are troubled with doubt about your faith? This is often a cause of soul-palsy. I am not going to utter idle denunciations of doubts, as though they were invariably a wilful sin; nay, I feel the truest sympathy for the doubter, where his doubts are honest, and bring trouble to his own soul, and are not the idle dreams of an unchastened fancy, or, what is worse, the sinful acceptance of doubt as a cloak for licentiousness of living. But, undoubtedly, a doubting spirit does destroy the brightness and vividness of faith, and paralyse the soul's best energies.

4. But it may be our natural disposition which makes us cold-hearted. God makes not all alike, and some are naturally less excitable and less impressionable than others. Well, if any one can honestly say, "I believe I am by constitution cold, and unable to feel as deeply and keenly as many others," and if, saying this, he mourns that it is so, and would thankfully kindle in himself warmer feelings of love and devotion, if he could, surely we may speak comfortably to such an one. We would say to him, "Religious emotion is no real test of grace. It is very blessed and a great help when God vouchsafes it; but it is no proof of holiness. Obedience is the only real test. "Hereby do we know that we love Him if we keep His commandments." Go on, simply obeying God's will—simply doing what you know to be pleasing to Him. It may be you may never experience any great amount of religious emotion; but you will gradually learn to love God better. As you go, you will be healed. The true way to look at religious emotion seems to be this: It is a blessed help in surmounting the first great difficulties of a life of repentance; it is a solace to the weary traveller—a spring of refreshment to the parched lip—an earthly foretaste of heavenly joy. But it must not be trusted in as the sign and evidence of a state of favour with God. Warm affections, deep emotions, love and joy and peace,—these are blessings to thank God for; but they are not necessary. Obedience is. So let none despair because he cannot arouse himself to great fervour of emotion. It may be that what you take for paralysis is but a colder constitution, and that you are nearer to your Saviour than you think.

I do not mean that you should be content with cold, dull feelings; nay, strive all you can after more warmth of love, more generosity of affection. But, if God denies you these graces, still cleave to Him in humble trust and hope. Obey now, and the joy and peace may be hereafter.

And now, before we end, a word about the healing. Aye, but first we must get to the Healer; and that is just what the poor paralysed soul finds so hard. Well, look at the poor paralytic in the Gospel. No one seemed more utterly shut out from the great Healer than he did. There he was, helpless, motionless, borne on his pallet by his four kind friends, but wholly unable to reach the presence of Christ. Yet he *did* reach it. Ah! yes, for no obstacle shall keep him back. The house may be full, the doorway thronged, the crowd impenetrable; but there are the outside stairs; there is the roof; there are ropes to be had; the roof must even be broken away. It is a bold, strange way to take. But anything to get to Jesus. Yes, my friends, rest not for one moment—care not what violence you use. He loves the gracious violence of importunity. It was once said, "The Kingdom of Heaven suffereth violence, and the violent take it by force." This means that men would not be kept out, in their eager vehemence of desire to enter the kingdom of the Messiah. Emulate their vehemence; overcome every impediment. Ah! may it not be that one reason why you find it so hard to get to your Saviour is that you are *too low down*? You want to go up higher, to mount the stairs of prayer and praise and holy adoration. Or, perchance, it is that you want to go down lower—to let yourself down with the cords of penitence and humiliation and confession and contrition, down to the very dust, before the feet of Jesus. *Then* it will come—the pardon, the release, the cure. Oh, blessed souls! if only to you is spoken the word of healing, "Arise, take up thy bed, and go unto thine house!" Oh! what joy, to arise with new life and vigour and health and energy!—to feel the old chains fall off!—to know that, even as in calling and baptismal grace ye are risen with Christ from the dead, so in the power of a Divine renewal ye can claim your baptismal standing and say, "I am risen indeed with my risen Lord;" "I live; yet not I, but Christ liveth in me!" Oh! blessed resurrection! How bright, how free, how happy, how heavenly, is now our life! Yes, but the restored paralytic has two things to do; and ye too, dear friends, when Christ sets you free from your bonds, will also have two things to do. He must take up his bed, and he must go to his house. He must take up his bed: he has a burden to carry, even when he goes away cured. And you—yes, there is a cross for you. And one burden you have to bear is the bed on which you have lain. The very sloth and apathy, the very coldness and deadness, in which you have been lying, must be carried by you as a burden of past sin, never quite to be forgotten, as you go on your way. "My sin is ever before me," is the penitent's confession. And even though able now to bear away your old sin, which once bore you as its victim to destruction, yet it may be the shoulder has yet to chafe under the burden. And then the going to his house. It sounds so common-place! Nothing heroic to do! Not even "Come, follow Me." Only "Go unto thine house." Yes, beloved brethren, it is in very truth to your common daily unromantic life and occupations that God sends you back. You feel a little chill of disappointment. It were so pleasant to do some great thing for your dear Lord. Well, He has a great thing for you to do—a great thing, though to be done amidst little things; for it is a great thing to one who has been cold and dead to be warm with holy love and alive to the things of Heaven. And this is your task. And I think it is sometimes a greater thing to live a Heavenly life in the midst of common things and ordinary duties, in spite of all the depressing hindrances of worldly occupation and unsympathising companions, than to many it would be to give their all to some noble work or to leap into the flames of martyrdom.

V.

PRAYERLESSNESS,

BY THE

REV. J. ERSKINE CLARKE, M.A.,

Vicar of S. Andrew's, Derby.

Prayerlessness.

1 SAMUEL xii., 23.

Samuel said, "As for me, GOD forbid that I should sin against the Lord in ceasing to pray for you."

And in COLOSSIANS i., 9, 10,

S. Paul says, "For this cause, we also, since the day we heard it, do not cease to pray for you, and to desire that ye might be filled with the knowledge of His will in all wisdom and spiritual understanding, that ye might walk worthy of the Lord unto all pleasing, being fruitful in every good work."

I AM desired to address you this morning on the subject—"Prayerless men, hindrances to the work of the Church in the world;" and I have chosen these two texts because they show how Samuel in the Old Testament times, and S. Paul in the New, shrank from being reckoned among the prayerless men.

Israel had sinned in asking Samuel to set a king over them, when the Lord God was their King. At the call of Samuel the Lord sent thunder and rain on the day of wheat harvest to show them that their wickedness was great. Then the people feared the Lord and Samuel, and all the people said unto Samuel, "Pray to the Lord thy God for us that we die not." And Samuel said, "Fear not, ye have done this great wickedness, yet turn not aside from following the Lord, but serve him with all your heart, for the Lord will not forsake His people. But as for *me*, God forbid that I should *sin* against God in ceasing to pray for you; but I will teach you the good and the right way.

If Samuel had ceased to pray for rebellious Israel, he would have become a hindrance to the work of the Church in the world, and would have *sinned* against God, as well as been unfaithful to the people, who looked up to him as their Judge and Priest.

S. Paul, writing to the faithful brethren in Christ at Colosse, tells them that since he had heard from Epaphras of their faith in Christ and love to all the saints he and his fellow-labourers had not ceased to pray for them, desiring especially that they might be filled with the knowledge of the will of God—that in all wisdom and spiritual understanding they might walk and behave in a manner worthy of that great and glorious God whose servants and worshippers they were, and that they might be fruitful in every good work.

If S. Paul and his fellow-servants *had* ceased to pray for the converts at Colosse, they would so far have become hindrances of the work of the Church and of Christ in the city of Colosse.

We see, then, from our texts that, alike for rebellious Israel and for God-fearing Colossians, the prayers of God's servants, Samuel and S. Paul, were offered without ceasing; that Samuel felt that to have ceased and become prayerless would have been to *sin* against God and to injure his countrymen; and that S. Paul felt that if the Colossians were to be fruitful in good *works*, he must not cease to *pray* for them.

Prayerlessness, then, hinders the work of the Church in the world. It hinders the rebellious from returning to God, and their allegiance to Him; it hinders the weak saints from becoming fruitful in good works; while prayer for others—intercessory prayer—furthers God's work in the world and brings down blessings on the brethren.

True, we cannot tell *how* this is. Sceptics may scoff at it; philosophers may scorn it; but there is some way beyond the present ken of our understandings whereby the determinate counsel and foreknowledge of God *is* consistent with the efficacy of our prayers to Him.

Let simple folk accept simply and hold firmly the words of Holy Writ—the precepts to pray, and the promises that God will hear and answer prayer! Our Lord would never have taught us to pray if prayer were useless. Our Lord would never have prayed Himself, as He so often did, if prayer were not acceptable to the Father.

Wherefore let not the simple-hearted be disturbed by the sophistries of those who boast themselves as wiser than the ancients. Let them believe their Bibles; let them believe the Church; let them believe with Tennyson—

> More things are wrought by prayer
> Than this world dreams of. Therefore let thy voice
> Rise like a fountain for me night and day.
> For what are men better than the sheep or goats
> That nourish a blind life within the brain,
> If, knowing God, they lift not hands in prayer,
> Both for themselves and them that call them friend?
> For so the whole round world is every way
> Bound by gold chains about the feet of God.

Or in the words of another—

> The salt preserveth the sea, and the saints uphold the earth:
> Their prayers are the thousand pillars that prop the canopy of Nature;
> Verily an hour without prayer from lips of some child of man
> Were a curse in the kalendar of Time—a spot of the blackness of darkness.

The prayerless man contributes nothing to the golden chains that bind the world to the footstool of God. He contributes nothing to the thousand pillars that uphold the earth. He contributes no single ray to lighten the darkness of this life. He is a non-conductor of Divine blessings.

He may be clever, learned, rich and active, kindly and benevolent; but he does not really confer so great blessings on mankind as the godly maid-servant who offers her pleading prayer from her garret, or the child that whispers in earnest the Lord's Prayer into the ear of God.

And it is well for some of us to remember that even the busy Church-worker, frequent at committee-meetings and the like, may not do as much for God as the invalid whose prayers go up for the work of the Church from the couch of pain and weakness—

Behold that fragile form of delicate, transparent beauty,
Whose light blue eye and hectic cheek are fed by the bale fires of decline;
All droopingly she lieth as a dew-laden lily.
Hath not thy heart said of her, Alas! poor child of weakness, —
Thou hast erred? Goliath of Gath stood not with half her strength,
For Seraphim rally at her side; and the Captain of that host is God.
And the seried ranks of evil are routed by the lightning of her eye;
For that weak fluttering heart is strong in faith assured:
Dependence is her might; and behold she prayeth.

Seeing, then, brethren, how great the power of prayer, why are men so prayerless?

Some, not likely to be represented in Church, are prayerless because they have said in their heart and with their lips, There is no God. Or, if they do not deny the being of God, they deny His moral providence and government; they deny a future state. Content to be like dogs, dead and done with, they deny the revelation which God has given as if it were no better than a cunningly-devised fable.

Such persons do not, and cannot, pray.

Others are prayerless from sheer carelessness and earthliness. Heaven is hid from their view, and earth contains all they desire. To get money and to spend it—to deck and adorn the body, to nurse it in sickness, to pamper it in health—to answer the question, "What shall we eat, and what shall we drink, and wherewithal shall we be clothed"—this engrosses their whole attention. The lusts of the flesh and the pride of life so absorb them that they do not pray.

Others do not pray because their lives are so stained with sin. They so sin against their consciences that they feel it irksome to put themselves consciously into the presence of God. They feel that their prayers are a mockery while they persist in wilful sin; and so they put off prayer, as they put off amendment, to a future season.

Others pray not because they are so self-contained and self-reliant that they do not realise their need. They are as God unto themselves.

A little child had finished its evening prayer, and turned to its father, a godless man, with the unexpected question, "Father, *I've* said my prayers. Have you said yours? Are you too big to pray?"

How many there are who think in their hearts—I'm too big to pray.

But others (ah! how many of *us*) are really prayerless, though they *say* their prayers.

They kneel down without thought, and utter pious falsehoods, in solemn language, to the truth-loving God. They are mere formalists, and draw nigh to God with their lips while their hearts are far from Him, and they insult Him with their prayerless prayers.

Others are prayerless from lack of excitement.

Their's is a religion of fits and starts. They begin in the spirit, but end in the flesh. Their religion depends on external excitement, not on internal principle; and it fails when these excitements cease. Their religion is like the tree without root, that soon withers, or like the land flood, which soon runs off, because it has no living stream to supply it.

How is it, then, with each of us, in the matter of prayer? For our own soul's sake let us see to it. If we pray not, we can have no hope. We refuse the one way by which alone our souls can live; for prayer is the Christian's vital breath—the Christian's native air—our watchword at the gates of death—we enter Heaven by prayer.

But my subject is, rather the effect of lack of prayer on the welfare of *others*—on the work of the Church.

By his irreligious spirit, by his evil example, the prayerless man depraves those amongst whom he lives. He frustrates efforts made to guide the young and ignorant into the ways of holiness. And, moreover, he does nothing to draw down the Divine blessings on the world and on the Church.

Be not ye, brethren, of the number of these prayerless men.

Pray ye for the *wicked* that forget God and pray not for themselves. We know that God heareth such prayers; for (as we read in Job xlii., 37) He said to Eliphaz and his two friends, "My wrath is kindled against you; but my servant Job shall *pray for you*; for him will I accept, lest I deal with you after your sins."

Samuel said that he dared not sin against God by ceasing to pray for rebellious Israel.

S. James says "That the effectual fervent prayer of a righteous man availeth much."

And pray also and specially for the servants and ministers of God, that they may be filled with the knowledge of His will and be fruitful in good works. Sometimes in Northern seaports scores of richly-laden vessels are lying in the river a few miles below the city, anxiously waiting to reach the wharves. Why are they delayed? Because the channel is closed with ice. Thus is it with the exceeding great and precious promises of God. He is waiting, and willing to bestow them; but even He cannot bestow them, because the appointed channel is not open, by which God is pleased to communicate them to us, and by which we receive His blessings.

Wherefore, let *us* pray that the work of God's Church may not be hindered by our restraining our supplications.

If in our consciences we feel that our prayers have been formal and careless, let us seek the gift of God's Spirit; for when God pours His Spirit on a man, then man will pour out his spirit before God. The breath of prayer comes from the life of faith; and, if we have not the spirit of prayer, let us begin with the spirit of confession and the spirit of praise; so that our faith may be quickened, and thus our prayers may become more real and sincere.

And, if we *do* pray somewhat, let us seek for more of what the Yoruba Christians call "the gift of the knees"—the spirit of prayer!

Bishop Hall saith, "An arrow, if it be drawn up but a little way, goes not far; but, if it be pulled up to the head, it flies swiftly and pierces deep." Thus prayer, if it be dribbled forth from careless lips, falls at our feet. It is not the *arithmetic* of our prayers, how many they be; nor the *rhetoric* of our prayers, how eloquent they be; nor the *geometry* of our prayers, how long they be; nor the *music* of our prayers, how sweet our voice may be; nor the *logic* of our prayers, how argumentative they be; nor even the *Divinity* of our prayers, how good the doctrine may be, which God cares for; but it is fervency of spirit that availeth much. It is not so much the length as the strength of prayer that is needed; not so much the labour of the lip as the travail of the soul.

It is a tradition of the British Army that the Infantry when in squares has never given way before a foe; and when formed in squares the front rank steady themselves on one knee. Let us, who aim to carry the truth of God into the enemy's midst, steady ourselves on *both* knees, and by prayer let us wrestle from the Everlasting a blessing upon our work.

How few, in this restless age, practice in their prayer the seven times a-day of David—the three times a-day of *set* prayer and giving of thanks of Daniel—the praying to God always of Cornelius—the waiting on God continually; and, therefore, few triumph in the Lord—few know the joy of true content; and many a good work in the Church fails and languishes because men are prayerless and faint-hearted, and do not besiege Heaven with prayer, so that the Lord may open the gates of Heaven, and pour down His blessing from on high.

VI.

INTEMPERANCE,

BY THE

VEN. J. SANDFORD, B.D.,

ARCHDEACON OF COVENTRY, AND RECTOR OF ALVECHURCH.

Intemperance.

1 SAMUEL, xvii., 29.

"Is there not a cause?"

To enlighten, reform, and elevate their fellow-creatures, and thus to make them good and happy, has been the aim of righteous and heroic men in every age of the world, and never more notably than in our own.

All honour, therefore, to those, whether associated or single-handed, who, without the patronage of the great or even the countenance of religious bodies, have withstood in any place the Moloch of intemperance, which has inflicted more evil and brought more shame on our fatherland than any other cause whatever.

Such benefactors of their species toiled, not long ago, one or two in a parish—a few, it might be, in a city—or, as obscure societies, in different parts of the country—to call the attention of the Legislature, and the magistracy, and the clergy, and other notables in our land, to what was working such deadly mischief in our midst; and those whom they addressed, for the most part, stood aloof from them, and pooh-

poohed them, and regarded them as childish, and officious, and fanatical.

As with every great movement in this country, the cause of Temperance began in weakness and obscurity, and struggled with contempt, and was ridiculed and laughed at.

But it was the cause of suffering humanity; and when education spread, and reading was diffused, and religion revived, and multitudes awoke to a sense of what God and Society require at every man's hand, this state of thoughtlessness and apathy could exist no more. Good and sensible men could not but perceive that a vice which degraded, and embruted, and pauperised the population—which caused so much distress and crime, and wrecked the peace of families, and retarded industry, and increased the public burdens, and filled our gaols and poor-houses and lunatic asylums, and impaired the efficiency of our armies and our fleets—was not a thing to be overlooked or trifled with. And of late the question before us to-night has assumed its due importance; and all who wish well to their country, and well to religion, are beginning to inquire as to the extent of the mischief, and as to the manner in which it is to be coped with; and a great authority has pronounced that "publicans' profits represent mis-spent money, and that this is the great point to be recognised on both sides."

There is, in fact, a growing conviction that health, and economy, and national progress of any sort, are incompatible with intemperance. The Nation is prepared to go into the facts, conscious that it has a solemn duty in connection with them—that to treat intemperance as irremediable is at once criminal and suicidal—that, unless we grapple with it, the crimes and the miseries caused by it will be chargeable on ourselves.

As to the facts, they are patent and undeniable, and admitted by all who will look into the question. You have them in epitome in this volume—the Convocation Report—the result of minute and exhaustive inquiry, containing the testimonies of our judges, our magistrates, the heads of our police, our governors of prisons and masters of workhouses and medical authorities, throughout the kingdom, and the parochial clergy of the whole province of Canterbury. And, considering its contents and its cost, I may be permitted to say that it ought to be in the hands of every one interested in the welfare of his country.

Thank God! the National Church to-day is in the van of inquiry. Its clergy no longer treat intemperance as a question with which they have nothing to do. Our prelates are prepared to deal with it both in Parliament and on the platform. Our synods have already made, or are about to make it the subject of their anxious deliberation. Our noblest minsters and parish churches are opened for its discussion; and the incumbent of this parish,—with the manliness and large heartedness which distinguish him,—has allowed it to-night a place in his Octave and a voice in his pulpit.

My subject is—The evils of intemperance and its corrective; and I ask a candid hearing while I state them.

And first, the Evils of Intemperance. They are matters of public notoriety, matters of national statistics, known in every locality, and, alas! in multitudes of our homes. And pauperism, disease, lunacy, premature decay and death, domestic misery, atrocious crimes, are the fruits seen and read of all men, and which no one in this country now attempts either to deny or to extenuate.

Intemperance impairs the national strength. *Intemperance* obstructs the national trade. *Intemperance* degrades the national character. *Intemperance* has made the national name a bye-word amongst the peoples of the earth.

There is no country in the world so debased by drunkenness as our own! Neither amongst Hindoo, nor Buddhist, nor fire-worshipper, nor Mahometan (such was the testimony of Sir John Bowring to myself), is there anything approaching to the intemperance of our countrymen. "I have seen more drunkenness," said another witness on whom I could rely, "in six days in England, than during six months' journey across the continent of Europe."

Moreover, it is the complaint of Hindoo philanthropists now traversing the land, that their heathen compatriots learn drunkenness, and the vices to which it leads, from English Christians.

And in these days of wars and rumours of wars it may well claim attention, that there is nothing so destructive of the discipline or so injurious to the strength of our forces, both by land and sea, as intemperance. It demoralises and disintegrates our armies, and under-mans and endangers our navies, and covers our coast every winter with wrecks and with corpses.

Above all, *intemperance* degrades human nature; for it deprives man of that in which his real dignity consists—his reason and his self-respect. In the words of a truly noble advocate of the temperance cause (Thomas Barker), "it obliterates the lineaments of a high and Divine life, and sinks a being, created in the image of God, to the level of the brute, the savage and the fiend." We read of a people in ancient times who, in order to instil into their children an abhorrence of this revolting vice, used to exhibit their slaves in a state of intoxication. They set before them one of a degraded race, still more debased by the loathsome signs of inebriety. "Look," said they, "how drunkenness disfigures the human form divine. Observe the staggering gait, the unseemly gestures, the idiotic features of that creature. See how drunkenness disguises a man, un-mans a man, makes a man a beast! What can be more shocking or degrading? You see it makes a man more debased than a slave, sinks him below the level of a brute. Would you be like him?" And yet thus do Christian men degrade themselves in the sight of God, of angels, of their fellow-creatures. Thus do husbands degrade themselves in the eyes of their wives, fathers in the eyes of their children. Think of a wife, who has vowed at the altar to honour and obey her husband; think of little children, or of grown-up sons and daughters, who are bound to reverence theii parents, and who, in the person of a parent, ought to revere the image and authority of God Himself; think of such gazing on him who ought to claim their reverence and love, and train them in the nurture and the fear of God, outraging the sanctities of home and wallowing in intoxication!

Again, *intemperance* betrays men into the commission of the most revolting crimes. Look at the annals of guilt, or the diurnal statements of offences against society. Look at the police reports, or the trials at the sessions or assizes. Read the testimonies of our judges, or of the officers of justice in this volume. Recall the outrages against person and property that are recorded in every journal, or have come under your own immediate notice. Are they not almost all to be traced to excess in drink? Adultery, fornication, theft, embezzlement, strife, manslaughter; these are its fruits! How many a robbery, how many a murder, how many a suicide, has been committed at its instigation! How many a criminal when in the hands of justice, when expiating his crimes on the ignominious scaffold, has exclaimed, "It was drink that brought me here!" How many an unhappy mañiac has it confined within the walls of a mad-house! *Drink* makes the chaste man sensual, the honest man a thief, the mild man a fury, the humane man a murderer! When a man is in liquor the Spirit of God leaves him, and the Devil takes possession of him. He becomes a ready prey to diabolical suggestions, and is led captive by Satan at his will. He is hurried on to embrue his hands in a fellow-creature's blood or to turn them against his own life; and when he recovers from his frenzy and awakes from his stupefaction, and finds that he has lost his character, damaged his worldly prospects, incurred the penalties of the law, and has, perhaps, a scaffold to look to,—the conviction, which enters like iron into his soul, is this, "See to what drink has brought me."

In a word, the love of drink ruins both body and soul. No strength of constitution can long withstand the inroads of this destructive vice. It impairs the intellect, and abridges life, and brings on premature decrepitude, and makes young men old. It has slain more of our manhood than the sword ever did—more in one city in one year than fell on the field of Waterloo—more than all the natural diseases to which the frame of man is subject.

It is the source of half the misery and almost all the crimes that have filled the world with tears. Ask the officers of justice, ask our medical advisers, ask those who tend on lunatic asylums, ask the gaoler and executioner; and they will all confess, as they revolve the page of human misery and guilt, that intemperance is the great scourge of humanity—that the pothouse is the nursery of the hospital, the prison, the hulks, and the gallows!

It would, indeed, be easy to trace the progress of this dreadful vice through its successive stages of sin and degradation, till it terminates as I have described; and I should only rcall what your own experience would confirm.

Of all the fallacies that mislead men there never was a grosser than that the drunkard is no man's enemy but his own. He is not only miserable himself, but the cause of misery and ruin to all connected with him. No one can place any confidence in him, or have any peace with him. His vice renders him the pest of the neighbourhood in which he lives, and is the utter bane of domestic happiness. Farewell respectability, comfort, and peace in that dwelling of which the inmate is given to drink. As Archbishop Thomson graphically observed—"When drunkenness comes in at the door, happiness flies out at the window."

Yes! point out to me the dwelling of a drunkard, and I will draw for you the picture within—the wife wan, emaciated, and neglectful of her person; the children half-starved and in tatters; the apartments dingy, dirty, and despoiled of furniture; everything wearing an aspect of discomfort and desolation; everything proclaiming, "*This is the dwelling of a man given to drink.*"

Need I add to all this that intemperance obstructs the entrance of the Gospel and the work of the Church; that it thins our congregations, thwarts our clergy, is an utter foe to both morals and religion. To quote a few of my clerical correspondents:—"Sabbath-breaking, swearing, and drunkenness are vices that go together." "Intemperance keeps numbers from Church." "Persons who are addicted to intemperance rarely attend upon the ordinances of religion." "Intemperance keeps men from Church, and renders them indifferent to religion." "Practical atheism is produced by it." "People are hardened and brutalised by the constant spectacle of drunkenness." "Religion is at a discount," "public ordinances are despised, and Sunday is grossly neglected." Lastly, to quote one who is well entitled to speak, "the clergy everywhere, but in our large towns especially, are discouraged, cast down, almost driven to despair, through the universal prevalence of the vice of drinking, and the temptations that are multiplied for its encouragement on every hand under the protection of law. It thwarts, defeats and nullifies their Christian schemes and philanthropic efforts to such an extent that it is becoming a matter of grave question whether infidelity, religious indifference, and social demoralisation are not making head against us, in defiance of all our churches, our clergy, our Scripture-readers, and our schools."

How, in fact, can it be otherwise, when our people

are plied with legalised temptations on every side; when more than a hundred millions sterling are annually consumed in this country in intoxicating drink; when the liquor trade has assumed such gigantic dimensions that it beards the Legislature and defies both the power of the Government and the voice of public opinion!

But I can neither do justice to this branch of the subject nor exhaust it; and I have said enough, I trust, on it, to secure your sympathy and, it may be, your co-operation.

I will only add that I have not been handling it rhetorically or from hearsay; for I have gone into this question in all its details, seeking information wherever I could obtain it and conversing in our prisons with the unhappy criminals whom excess had brought there,—some of whom I sought out at the request of their friends, whom their excess had reduced from competence to penury. More than this, I have received the dying confession of one who committed murder and other atrocious crimes when inflamed by drink; have stood upon the felon's grave of one who, though the child of pious parents, was brought in early manhood to the scaffold by an act of drunkenness, in which he took the life of his bosom friend. And amongst the most painful recollections of my life are instances of self-destruction caused by drink, of which, as a pastor, I have had harrowing and multiplied experience. And when, in addition to all this, I ascertained that women of condition, and even ladies of fashion, are often the slaves of drink; when one of them, who on what she supposed her death-bed, had renounced this loathsome vice, expressing deep contrition, returned to what has since cast her from husband and from home, and reduced her to the level of the vilest of her sex, told me, when I put life and death before her, that she would risk her soul to indulge in drink; I felt that I had no alternative, all uncongenial as it was to my tastes and habits as a student and a pastor, but to set myself, even in the decline of life, to the task with which I have been recently engaged. And on this behalf I appeal confidently to my brethren of the English clergy and of the English laity. I know their aversion to anything like cant, or hyperbole, or sensational excitement. But I also know that, when their judgment is convinced and their hearts are touched, there is nothing in the way of effort or of sacrifice from which they will draw back.

And this brings me to my second head—the corrective or the remedy, and the spirit in which it must be applied.

And, first, we must diminish temptation—in other words, restrict the liquor trade. And remember the demand for this—as a leading journal, wise in its generation, significantly observes—"comes from the chief victims, or the working classes themselves." There is nothing new in what that journal says; but its utterance is ominous now, as coming from such a source, and may best be given in its very words—"They, the working classes, declare that the facilities for getting liquor in any quantity are so great that they amount practically to the encouragement of intemperance. A man, who might not care to walk half a mile to a public-house, would turn into one of half a dozen placed right in his way. The consumption of drink, as of all other articles, must be increased by bringing it home to every man's door. That is the assertion of those who know where the shoe pinches, and ask to be saved from the temptations they experience. If legislation, whatever be its form, does not restrict the expenditure upon intoxicating drinks, it will simply be a dead letter. If it does so, and according to the measure in which it does so, it will diminish the profits and damage the property of the liquor trade. . . . It is absolutely impossible to protect or advance the morality of the people without doing direct and proportionate injury to the liquor trade. . . . The wish of all thinking persons in this country is, that half the money now spent in drink should be spent in something better. Unless the new bill does this, or something towards it, it will be of no effect at all; and if it does as much, it will be open substantially to precisely the same objections on the part of the Trade as the bill of 1871.—(*Times*, Monday, September 4, 1871).

Such are the arguments of our leading journal, which, for reasons which I need not enunciate, is always a significant exponent of national opinion. As a legislative question I go beyond its present utterances, for I claim for the majority of the ratepayers themselves the power of restriction; and till this is granted there seems little likelihood of a satisfactory legislative settlement.

Secondly, there is the force of example. In former days I used to discourage, and even scout, what I now rely on, and utter what I now consider platitudes. In former days I had faith in schemes of education, and rational pastime, or innocent diversion, and more comfortable dwellings for the working classes, and other benevolent devices, as sufficient to wean men from public-houses and correctives to intemperance,—

in the efficacy of all which counter attractions, we are told by high authority, the liquor-dealers have as little faith as myself; and my sole argument with temperance advocates used to be that the Gospel received into the heart is the only and all-sufficient remedy for moral evil of every sort; and I was zealous in urging this, as some of you, no doubt, are in all sincerity, to-night.

But I have learnt that educated men, and literary men, and some of the most skilled and intelligent of our workmen—yes, and scholars and divines—may be the slaves of drink; and that the persons whom we want to reach seldom enter either places of harmless recreation or of worship, preferring to these the glare and the glee of the public-house, where they spend in vicious self-indulgence what might provide comforts, and even luxuries, for their families. I have cumulative and conclusive testimonies in this volume, from men of the largest practical experience and constantly in contact with the victims of intemperance—to wit, our constabulary and governors of prisons, and masters of workhouses—that with multitudes there is no power of self-restraint, and that for such total abstinence is the only cure; that before they can be taught self-respect, or brought within the reach of religion, they must be restrained from drink. And I have now no faith at all in moderation among habitual frequenters of public-houses, or on the part of any that have once been the slaves of intemperance.

It is, besides, a well-authenticated fact that such persons,—who have abandoned habits of total abstinence, when once adopted on conviction,—have generally been again entangled and overcome, and thier last state has been worse than the first.

And, therefore, for conscience sake, as an example to weaker brethren "for the present necessity," as S. Paul speaks, with a view to recover souls out of the snares of the devil, and for national reformation, I am an abstainer. I believe this to be the only stand point for a minister of religion, or, indeed, for any one who, like myself, would plead the cause of temperance with any prospect of success.

That alcohol may be useful as a stimulant, and, when medically prescribed, may even save life, I should be the last man to deny. But as long as alcohol is a narcotic poison,—and, even as a stimulant, only acts as a spur in the flank of a jaded horse,—to use it habitually as an article of diet is quite a different thing, as our medical men would be the first to admit; while, on the other hand, that abstinence from intoxicating drink is promotive of health, that it tends to impart vigour, and prolong life, is the experience of multitudes who have wrought hard and continuously without any stimulant whatever, and effected more without it than they could have done by its aid.

It was thus that the patriotic Cobden prosecuted his laborious mission—that the conqueror of Scinde achieved his triumphs in the East—that the heroic Havelock ran his career of glory. It may not be impertinent to add, as I do at the request of high medical authorities, that, had I not myself been in these later years an abstainer, I never could, at my time of life, have accomplished the task I had undertaken in connection with the question before us,—and that the stimulant, which was recently administered to me at the crisis of a dangerous disease, would in all probability have failed of its effects.

And if it be said that more can be effected for the national reformation by an example of moderation, I ask who are the men that plead the cause of temperance on our platforms and in our pulpits—that grapple with the destroyer of our people on every possible occasion—but the men who practise the noble self-denial commended by S. Paul, when he says, "If meat make my brother to offend, I will eat no flesh while the world standeth, lest I make my brother to offend?"

Brethren, would you redeem your fatherland from intemperance? Would you have the blessings of those who are ready to perish resting on you while you live, and gilding your graves when you die,—and restore peace and consolation to homes that are desolate and hearts that are breaking? You must abjure alcoholic drink, except when prescribed—just as arsenic or strychnine or any other poison may be—in minute quantities as a medicine.

And if you say that this is enthusiasm,—when, I would ask, was society ever redeemed without this? Who shall in any day wake a church or a people to a sense of duty, without a charge of enthusiasm? Were not Howard and Wilberforce, in their days, denounced as enthusiasts? And shall any who follow, however distantly, in the wake of these benefactors of their species escape the taunts of those who are too shallow-minded to appreciate their motives, and too worldly to follow their example? With what awful significance do the words of our Lord apply to this very question, when he says, "Except a man deny himself and take up his cross daily, and follow me, he cannot be my disciple."

Brethren! if I ever wish to be young again, it is

that I might traverse my fatherland with the message which you have heard from me to-night. There will be no lightening of its burdens, no reduction of its pauperism, no diminution of its crimes, no abatement of its miseries while it is enslaved by drink. Our schemes of national education, our dreams of moral and social reform, our plans for the enlightenment and amelioration of our people, our efforts at Church extension will come to nought, till the demon of intemperance is crushed beneath our feet.

VII.

WORLDLINESS,

BY THE

REV. G. C. HARRIS, M.A.,

PREBENDARY OF EXETER, AND VICAR OF S. LUKE'S, TORQUAY.

Worldliness.

ACTS xvii., 18.

"Then certain philosophers of the Epicureans and of the Stoics encountered him, and some said, 'What will this babbler say?' Others said, 'He seemeth to be a setter forth of strange Gods:' because he preached unto them Jesus and the Resurrection."

"WHEN we could no longer forbear, we thought it good to be left at Athens alone." To a mind so keen, so versatile, so large, so sympathetic, as S. Paul's, solitude must needs have been a trial; and this especially when the solitude was such as he means when, after sending back to his beloved Silas and Timotheus those who had brought him from Thessalonica, he remained by himself in Athens.

Now in what sense was S. Paul alone? In a great and crowded city, full of the most educated intellects of the day, the storehouse of the art-treasures of the world, the home of literature, and the shrine of poetry and tradition—in such a place how could S. Paul be alone? He was alone in the isolation of his soul, in the utter absence of sympathy with any of those among whom he found himself. Every principle that actuated his conduct was ignored or violated by the tendencies of thought and action around him. The concentrated worship of the One God with all the powers of man's being; the true and depreciatory sense of individual merit, coupled with the priceless value of the human soul; the probationary character of this life; the law of love from God to His creatures, and of sympathy between man and man; the need, the existence, of a personal Saviour; the life beyond the grave; the surrender of things present; the hope of things to come; all this was directly contradicted by the voluptuous idolatry or the philosophic speculations of Athenian life. It was, in fact, either "nonsense," which the worldly man would scorn, or it was a novel speculation, which the restless spirit of free inquiries viewed half with defiant incredulity, half with a hopeless longing that it might be true, that presented itself to the Athenian mind when Paul, alone in his belief against the world around, "preached unto them Jesus and the Resurrection."

For his "soul was stirred within him," knowing what was at stake. And pitying the souls of men, and feeling that he had the answer to all their questions, the remedy for all their ills, he spoke to one and another of that knowledge-loving crowd, as they loitered around the philosophic haunts or thronged the busy forum; and amid all the monuments of their ancestral glory, and the deathless triumphs of their national arts, he recognised among themselves the unconscious confession of their spiritual needs, and selected a vantage ground on their own territory on which to do battle with his bitterest foes.

They were "certain philosophers of the Epicureans and of the Stoics" which "encountered him." We may leave out of the question the other influences which hindered the work of the Church as represented by

S. Paul. The religion, so-called, of Athens, in which it abounded, could afford no real opposition to the soul-awakening appeals of the Gospel. It was falling already before the assaults of philosophy. Men who could think discarded the old superstitions; and though the altars of a thousand deities might smoke on every hand, and every public building be the temple of some presiding deity and every hearth be a domestic shrine, yet the characters of the gods whose history was embalmed in their legends was the strongest argument against their worship; and man with an immortal soul would crave something larger, greater, better than himself, if he is to worship anything at all. Thus the city, while it retained with duteous love the traditions of the past, was eagerly gathering from every land, with a sort of despairing curiosity, the offers of the most varied worship; and even the personifications of qualities of the soul and mind, Faith, Fortitude, Truth and Justice were beginning to have their altars, as if men were stretching out their desires to, at least, a standard of moral and mental improvement. But all would not satisfy. The worship of cold abstractions can kindle no enthusiasm; and in the despair of anything which their own experience had as yet discovered they raised their altar still "to the unknown God."

But philosophy had no such weaknesses. The Greek sage confidently told men to look in on themselves and find or frame their own chief good. I need not remind you there were many sects. But two only demand our present attention. "Certain philosophers of the Epicureans and of the Stoics encountered him." There were greater schools, which have left more lasting marks upon human thought;

but they rather prepared the way for Christianity. These two, however, contain in their principles so much of the wisdom that "is earthly, sensual, devilish"—so much that commends itself to the intellect and the passions of unreclaimed humanity—so much of the most successful state-craft of the Prince of this world—that we can easily see the lesson that underlies the statement that philosophers of these schools "encountered" S. Paul. In them and in him we have the chosen champions of the world and of the Church. In their encounter we have one typical incident in that deadly struggle, which can never end till the world itself shall have crumbled into ruin at the word of the Church's Lord.

Now let us note the combatants, and examine their tactics. The Epicureans were virtually Atheists. They did acknowledge the existence of some of the old gods of mythology; but they mocked their characters, and they denied their influence. The soul was to them but a part of the body, scarcely less material than its earthly dwelling-place. Death was to each man the end of all things. The body perished; the soul was scattered by decomposition into the elements of the world. Life was a short period, into which was to be compressed the greatest amount of indolence, leisure, or of sensual enjoyment. Chance was the only and the relentless directing power; and their creed was contained in brief in S. Paul's words, "Let us eat and drink, for to-morrow we die."

Their place of gathering was a garden near the Agora, or great market-place, at Athens; and there, with everything that was beautiful around them, they formed the pursuit of present ease and enjoyment into a system which was called philosophy. Self-advantage was the only motive; vice was to be shunned when it caused uneasiness; and trouble and ills should be ignored or avoided rather than overcome. In one word, they were the votaries of *pleasure*.

But there was the other school. Along the Agora, where S. Paul resorted daily, was a long colonnade or portico; and in this porch or "stoä" met another school of philosophers—the Stoics. Their creed was different. Wrapped in the mantle of their own self-esteem they scorned all the conditions of mortal life. They lived; and that was all they thought worthy their own recognition. Deity there was; but He was but revealed in all the world around them. Creative power he had none. He impressed form upon matter eternal as Himself; and wherever existence was, there was in it the Deity. They were Pantheists. They degraded God to the level of identity with the material world around them; and as they degraded God they exalted themselves. Calm in the assumed majesty of their own perfection, they held pleasure and pain to be alike contemptible. Life might have terrors for them if they were too weak to grapple with its ills; but death had none. Their soul at death was either destroyed; burned, some of them imagined; or else it was absorbed into the Deity—that is, into the material universe, which to them was God. Picture to yourselves, my brethren, if you can, on your day of mutual joy and Christian congratulation, these stony-hearted men. No sense of Nature's beauty filled them with enjoyment; no tale of heroism thrilled them with admiration; no note of sorrow ever woke an echo of sympathy in their souls. If they looked out of themselves, they saw nothing in man that drew them nearer to him; they saw nothing which they recognised as God that had a nature superior to their own. Isolation forbade them to "rejoice with them that do rejoice, or to weep with them that weep." Pantheism showed them nothing that could claim their homage as God. For all, themselves, and the nature round them, were but so many varying manifestations of the same universal essence.

Hence they stood, each separated from their fellows—each ignoring the claims of submission to God—on the pedestal of *their pride.*

Pleasure and Pride, then, in the persons of these philosophers, encountered S. Paul alone at Athens. What did he oppose to them? "Jesus and the Resurrection."

Jesus—that is, God—One and incarnate. He preached God in His unity, strictly separate from the manifold forms of pseudo-theology, which held out their pretensions on every side. He declared the true connection between God and man, not arrived at by degrading God to the level of the brute—nay, to the sharing a common nature with the things of earth, and air, and sea; but the recognition of the One Eternal God; proclaiming Him the Lord of the spirits of all flesh—Creator of all things visible and invisible; yet assuming the nature of man, and raising, purifying, ennobling, consecrating that nature by so doing; redeeming man from that curse of which even Grecian lore found many a fanciful explanation as it recognised its existence in all the changes and chances of this mortal life; redeeming him and opening before him a career which had Heaven for its goal, and perfection for its ultimate condition. He preached Jesus, too,—not only God, but man; and, as man, showing by His example how the redemption He offered was to be won; the perfect man—the one example—overcoming the world, but overcoming it by love—conquering, by the ingrafting of His own holy nature, all evil in the lives of men—teaching them to trample mercilessly on their lusts and passions, to deny themselves, to aim after happiness in another world instead of this, and yet to be possessors of a peace here which the world can neither give nor take away; Jesus, emphatically as an example, not *solely* a teacher, not merely one who thought and then said, "Do this," while I watch you; but one who did—nay, who suffered, willingly Himself, and *then* said, "Follow me." And he spoke to them also of that which gives force to the precepts of Jesus and meaning to this present life. He told them of the Resurrection. Oh, common subject! oh, familiar word! But how must it have thrilled in the hearts of these, his hearers, when it was boldly and plainly said to them that death was but a moment of transition, and the real life was then beginning—a life in which that which is always longing here might attain its desire—in which certainty will succeed to doubt, knowledge to ignorance, safety to temptation—where "the wicked cease from troubling, and the weary are at rest," not in the cold stillness of the grave, but in the blessed expectation of Paradise. And also, as involved in this idea, or, rather, flowing from the two—Jesus and the Resurrection—he told them how God would "judge the world by that man whom He had appointed," and how, therefore, this life became no longer a time of brief and thoughtless sojourn, where all the care of each succeeding moment was to make it merry as it sped, nor yet a field, where each man ruled supreme, owning no sovereignty but the dictates of his own heart and will; but rather a working-place, a time of trial, an exercise ground—not of ingenuity or strength, not of taste nor insensibility, but of truth and love, of humility and faith. How think you, brethren, that these doctrines pleased the luxurious Epicurean or the cold, proud Stoic? The doctrine of the Cross was to the Greek foolishness, and he neglected it for his pleasure, or he laughed it to scorn in his pride.

And, brethren, in the present day, wherever Paul is preaching, there will encounter him "certain philosophers of the Epicureans and of the Stoics." The same evil influences reproduce themselves in opposition to the work of Christ. They hinder His work when it is hindered in your souls as individuals; they encounter those who stand alone in the great battle-field of life, who wish to preach Jesus and the Resurrection, as their strength and hope, to those among whom, we must own, there is for all practical purposes but "an unknown God."

For, I say, what is the real hindrance to the Church's work, to the work of God, in your own hearts and lives, brethren, and in the general work? What is it really that paralyses exertion, or diverts attention, or intercepts the means for prosecuting the great campaign for conquering souls for Christ?

It is the same, brethren, as encountered S. Paul—pleasure and pride. They are still the two great forces of the world. They showed bravely, it is true, on the height of the Acropolis, amid the splendid statues of the market-place or the plane trees of the garden, where lust and beauty openly hunted the souls of men, or pride nursed them as the darlings of the world. Yes, it was the attractive side of sin that there blazed forth to dazzle and to scorch. And you would say that very different from the Athenian sky is the close atmosphere of the crowded towns, where the chief struggle of the Church must lie. No sculptor's art, no poet's song, throws a halo round the vices of the Haymarket, or the outrages of the Commune; and it is with such as these we have to deal. True, my brethren, I have spoken to you of Athens —of all the classic haunts of the most favoured spot of the heathen world. I have shown you, however, in that only the pleasant side of sin. Sweep away the garden and the portico, the marble and the gold; hush into silence the orator's voice and the poet's song; bring the matter from the distant pages of history, where the gloomiest crimes often shine with a borrowed light; bring the matter from Greece and antiquity; bring it to the present day and the commonplace; bring it to your own hearts, brethren; and if then there is anything that chills your sympathy, that holds it back from caring whether Christ's Church or the present world be victor in the strife, it is still the same as it was of old—pleasure and pride encounter you—Pleasure, with all its effeminacy and self-indulgence; pleasure, with its studied consideration of taste, and ease, and excitement; pleasure, in its purple and fine linen, faring sumptuously every day, while Lazarus, not hated but forgotten, is starving at the gate; pleasure, which lavishes on a present for a favourite a sum that would support a missionary for a year, or on a night of enjoyment that which would feed a starving family; pleasure, that thinks of the present and would drive the future far away as an unpleasant possibility, and asks for nothing more but to be left unchecked by word of warning or tale of sorrow "to live without God in the world." And pride, too, gives us a hardened heart—a heart steeled against entreaty, a quiverful of refusals to any appeal. There is the man who marches stately in the path of this life. Not like the votary of pleasure, immoral, or self-indulgent, or frivolous, or forgetful, he is correct in his outward conduct; he defies the world to cast an imputation on his character; he even affects to despise those who, professing religion, fall, as fall they must. If he owns a God—nay, start not, my brethren, at the height to which human audacity will soar—if he owns a God, it is one of his own making, a creature of his own, a being that in his heart he despises. In his philosophy he circumscribes the attributes of his God; he limits His powers; he explains His nature; he banishes Him from His Word, His Church, His Sacraments; he would keep Him a prisoner within the limits of human thought, while he denies Him the power to regulate His own laws or to fulfil His own promises. Oh, save us from this dreary Pantheism—from this cruel system, which leaves us without a single woe alleviated, a single tear-drop dried, a single difficulty explained; which leaves us without any being to look up to, no Almighty Father watching over His children in love, with nothing but an abstract being brought within the compass of our senses in the shape of a world inferior to the mind which contemplates it; nothing but a cold isolation, which makes each man a God unto himself, with no thought for another's weal or woe.

And if we drive the question backward—back from the luxurious drawing-room or the scholar's retreat; back from the comfortable home or the profitable shop; back from the realms of fashion, where hearts, happiness, lives, principles are bartered for place, or title, or position, or fortune; back from the expensive habits of polished society or the vice which calls itself respectable; back to the dark alley and the crowded court, "where the filthy bye-lane rings to the shriek of the trampled wife,"—brethren, it is in another form that the same hideous pair of twin evils, to which we too often are slaves, are lording it there. See pleasure in the flaring gin palace, the bloated drunkard, or that poor creature with the faded finery and the hectic cheek; see pride in the reckless villain, who tells you plainly—and there are thousands such—that he believes in neither God nor Devil, neither Heaven nor Hell, and that what his passion covets or his will demands, nothing but want of opportunity shall stop him from attaining.

And, amid this all, what is the antidote to the evil? While worldliness with its thorny growth is choking the produce of the good seed and preventing that perfection of fruit which marks the saintly life, what has the Church to offer in opposition? Still the same means as the great Apostle relied on at Athens—Jesus and the Resurrection. Pride may scorn the idea of faith; pleasure may rebel against the very notion of self-denial; the world in its wisdom may mock at the "babbling" of the Gospel, and in its habitual selfishness may reprobate the strangeness of any religion that really necessitates the Cross. But we know no new thing. The good news of the birth, the life, the death of Christ, is eighteen centuries old. In an age as busy, among intellects as keen, against opposition as bitter, amid thought as licentious and vice as fashionable as S. Paul confronted at Athens, we still, as he did, in a power not our own, preach forth Jesus and the Resurrection. It is the mission of the Church now, as it has ever been, to hold up the Cross in the face of that world that slew her Lord, and dare it to be indifferent. Jesus and the Resurrection; the example of Jesus, the meek and lowly, as the corrective to our swelling pride; the thought of the Resurrection as the touchstone of every undertaking. And not only the example and the thought, but the presence and the power. Again and again let it be repeated—the secret of the Christian's guidance and safety in this world is, life in the presence of Christ—that presence, which *is* ours, and which we in our recklessness carry from the font into the treacherous maze of life; nay—dare I say it? can anything but painful conviction of the existence of such an evil justify me in saying it?—which we carry from the Altar, where He gave Himself to us, back to the world which hates Him, or at the best returns His love with cold unconcern; not that we may leaven it, but that it may gather us into the throng, where those who say they love Him, and those who do not deny they despise Him, may be mingled in an undistinguishable crowd. But the presence of Jesus *is* ours, dear brethren, around us, in us. It not only surrounds us to remind us and rebuke us; it dwells in us to strengthen us and to comfort us. And the power of the Resurrection, too—not only the hope, but the power. The daily death to sin and self is complemented by the daily rising to newness of life. In the thought of the Resurrection the Quickening Spirit enables us to sit in judgment on act and motive; in the power of the Resurrection the Risen Lord, who is the Head of the Church, raises His members daily from that dying world which lieth in wickedness. Are these hard or unreal words? There is no subject on which it is easier to be unreal, or harder to be too hard, than this. The world *is* the sworn foe of Christ and His Church—deadlier to His children when she smiles than when she frowns. But ever let the thought of that loving eye which melted Peter when he sat among the servants round the fire be present with us, and much of the glamour of the world will fade away. Grasp with unrelaxing faith the last words of the Church's creed—"I look for the resurrection of the dead, and the life of the world to come;" and then there will be no hesitation, no lack of meaning, in the fervour of that prayer—"From all the *deceits* of the WORLD, the Flesh, and the Devil, good Lord, deliver us."

VIII.

LUKEWARMNESS,

BY THE

REV. W. R. CLARK, M.A.,

PREBENDARY OF WELLS, VICAR OF TAUNTON,

AND RURAL DEAN.

Lukewarmness.

REV. iii., 15, 16.

"I know thy works, that thou art neither cold nor hot: I would thou wer't cold or hot. So then, because thou art lukewarm, and neither cold nor hot, I will spue thee out of my mouth."

THOSE who believe that these seven Churches of Asia represent seven successive ages in the history of the Church have, undoubtedly, some apparent grounds for their opinion, even if we cannot allow that it rests upon a solid foundation. The age after that of the Apostles is not unfitly represented by the Church of Ephesus, which had left its first love. The prophecies respecting the times immediately preceding the second advent of our Lord would lead us to expect some such state of things as existed in the Church of Laodicea.

A large number of those who advocate the prophetical interpretation of these seven Epistles believe that the coming of Christ is very near at hand, and, consequently, that we have now entered the Laodicean age. It may possibly be, although I should be inclined to doubt it, that lukewarmness is the prominent feature in the religious character of the present age. No age is competent to judge of its own faults or virtues. But whatever may be the truth on this subject it will hardly be doubted that lukewarmness is a very common vice of our own day, and that it is a charge to which many of us are liable. At a time when education and civilisation have made great progress, when men are tempted to overlook the Divine Cause and Source of every blessing in the material results, there is a peculiar danger of the well-disciplined spirit of moderation degenerating into the vice of lukewarmness. In days when a large portion of men's thoughts is given to temporal prosperity and advancement and to outward display, the ardour of the pursuit of wealth and influence is very likely to beget lukewarmness about the things of God. It may be well for us, then, to study with deep prayerfulness and with earnest self-application the solemn lessons of this passage.

These words are some of the most impressive and awful in the whole Bible, whether we consider the class of persons to whom they are addressed, the character which they condemn, or the terrible expressions in which that condemnation is conveyed.

I will ask you to consider with me, by God's help, these three points:—1, the character of lukewarmness; 2, what we are to think of it; and, 3, how we are to deal with it.

I. *The character of lukewarmness.*

There is no definition needed of the word itself. It is simple and intelligible enough. The lukewarm is neither hot nor cold. It has not the fervour of true and deep devotion to God, nor yet the coldness of absolute enmity to Him. But although the word requires neither definition nor explanation, there is need of some caution in judging of the existence or absence of the character, and some points connected with it may usefully be dwelt upon.

Great mistakes are made about this character. Violence and impetuosity are sometimes mistaken for fervour in the service of God when they really proceed from quite another cause, and are lying side by side in the same nature with lukewarmness and religious indifference. Moderation is sometimes set down as lukewarmness, when it springs out of the deepest devotion to God and receives its temper from love to Him and charity towards man. Vehemence of spirit and of speech may proceed from the fervour of sincere and deep devotion to God; but it may also proceed from natural impetuosity of disposition, and from a hot zeal for one's own party and opinions. A man may be a warm partisan and a very bad Christian. He may be a fierce controversialist, with little real zeal for truth, for the glory of God, or the good of man.

On the other hand, a sanctified moderation may be mistaken by unspiritual men for lukewarmness in the cause of God. Moderation is, however, no more a proof of lukewarmness than violence is a proof of loving zeal and fervent devotion. Self-control and self-denial, a giving-up of one's own will, and a consideration for the wishes and the well-being of others, are as much Christian duties as fidelity to the truth and earnestness in making it known. A true and Christian moderation—a moderation which is not cold and lukewarm, but which is loving and devout—is one of the most precious and beautiful fruits of the Holy Spirit of God.

We must go deeper if we would understand the real nature and bearings of the evil spirit of lukewarmness.

1. It is a spirit which is *deficient in the great Christian graces of faith, and hope, and love.* Instead of being controlled by the powerful Divine influence of faith, its chosen guide is prudence. For the Christian grace of hope it bases its expected future upon a mere calculation of probable consequences. Of course it knows little of love as a mainspring of action. Instead of this greatest of the gifts of God, it follows the dictates of self-interest or of common sense, or perhaps it is directed by a vague sense of duty. In any case its favourite maxim is, "Above all, no zeal."

2. Then, again, the lukewarm are *satisfied with a very low standard of life.* To such the ideal of the Gospel seems to be quite unattainable, or, at the least, an object which they neither hope nor desire to attain. They delight to quote the words of the *Christian Year,* although they use them in a very different sense from that which was intended by their saintly author. They will not "strive to wind themselves too high for sinful men beneath the sky," nor do they appreciate the great Christian watchword of progress. It may, perhaps, be suitable for an Apostle who had renounced the world and the things of the world to forget the things which are behind, and to press onwards to those which are before. Growth in grace may be a beautiful aspiration for men who are aiming at the perfection of the saints, but not for them. They are contented with something short of this. They don't think of pretending to be better than their neighbours. The average common sense religion, which suits the average man of the world, is good enough for them. They go so far as to fear that people who profess more are either hypocrites or

enthusiasts. A great deal of this has a very plausible sound. It sometimes imposes upon unthinking minds. There can be no doubt that such language often arises from a deep self-deception on the part of those who use it.

3. Observe another feature in this character. It is *destitute of all real and earnest devotion.* And this is true, whatever meaning of that word we may adopt.

(1.) The lukewarm are either negligent or perfunctory in their use of Divine ordinances. They commonly neglect them, caring little for them, and making little use of them. They do not actually leave off prayer; but they spend as little time over it as they possibly can. The Bible is not altogether unread, and it is not treated with open disrespect. But it is little used, and is never a constant and valued companion. The Holy Communion may not be entirely neglected. It is often virtually so; but in many cases it would not be thought decent to neglect a duty which others perform. It would not be respectable; and the lukewarm character aims at respectability. But if these various duties are recognised they are placed in a position quite secondary to one's own convenience or one's worldly engagements. If the two things at any time seem to clash, it is the world which has the preference.

And even when such duties are not neglected, they are performed in a cold, listless, and perfunctory manner. The lukewarm may say their prayers; but they do not pray earnestly, trustfully, hopefully. They read their Bibles, but it is not in the spirit of one who says, "Speak, Lord; thy servant heareth." It is not with the eagerness of one who is seeking for hidden treasure. They go to the altar of God, but it is not to "the God of their joy and gladness." There is no earnest, searching, self-examination before their approach; there is no hungering and thirsting after righteousness as they prepare to receive the bread of life; there is no joyful lifting up of the head after they have drunk of the brook by the way.

2. Nor is their devotion greater in the way of practical well-doing. This is more surprising. The lukewarm are apt to boast that they are practical men, and not theorists. They have no high-flown notions of religion. They do not profess to know anything of the self-abasement which cries out, "God be merciful to me, a sinner;" of the longing desire which exclaims, "Like as the hart desireth the water-brooks so longeth my soul after Thee, O God;" of the rapture which says, "To me to live is Christ, and to die is gain." But they may boast, they imagine, of their devotion to practical duties. Like many other boasts, this one of theirs is false. They are as destitute of sincere devotion in the practical life as in the contemplative—in the side which is turned towards men as in that which turns towards God.

Speak to them of work which may be done for the glory of Almighty God, or the good of men, and they will tell you that they are not sure that any good can be done. If it can, they feel sure—and here perhaps they are not so far wrong—that they are not the people to do it. At any rate they will make no considerable sacrifice for it. Zeal asks, What can I do? Its chief difficulty is not in finding a disposition for work, but in finding occasions for exercising it. Lukewarmness evades every demand made upon its devotion. It asks not how much can it do, but how little. If a duty is pressed home upon it, it discovers, after mature consideration, that it is not bound to do it. Even if it cannot altogether deny the duty, it seeks and finds quite easily abundant excuses for neglecting it.

You ask for a sacrifice of its time; but its time is entirely occupied in other business. It might like to be more diligent in the use of Divine ordinances, more active in works of benevolence, of charity, of mercy; but it has no time for them, although it has plenty for pleasure, for relaxation, for doing its own will.

You ask for money to be spent in the building of churches or of schools, in sending missions to the heathen abroad, or to the heathen at home. It has money; but it spends it all in more necessary work, or it does not see any use in promoting the objects for which its interest is solicited. It is the same with its ease and leisure. It may admit, with a languid acquiescence, that all that we are and all that we have are of God, belong to Him, and should be consecrated to Him. In practice His claims are disregarded and His demands are ignored.

Such was the character which was predominant in the Church of Laodicea, and which is found very widely among ourselves. Such is the character to which our blessed Lord calls our attention in this epistle. Let us ask, under the guidance of His solemn words,

II. *What are we to think of this character?*

What does the world think of it? What does it think of itself? What does our Lord think of it?

1. The world generally thinks well of it. It is

one of the world's chief favourites. And this is quite intelligible. It has some merits. It is frequently distinguished by a fair average consistency of deportment. It has not a high standard, so that it is in less danger of falling below it. Besides, it aims at respectability, and is a little sharp on the failings of those who profess more, or aim at more than itself. Then it is reasonable and moderate in its demands, and gives other people little trouble, neither rebuking them by its theories nor shaming them by its practice. The world can hardly fail to like it, since it adopts the principles and rules and maxims of the world, and not those of Jesus Christ.

It has been remarked that of all the seven Churches of Asia there were only two which were free from persecution in some form or shape—Sardis and Laodicea. They were the two worst. Sardis had a name that it lived, and was dead. Laodicea was apparently prosperous, but was lukewarm. The world and the devil let them alone. They were their friends: it was safer not to disturb them. It is the same now. The lukewarm really belong to the world and not to Christ, although they may profess His name; and the world loves its own. This is a character which it holds in special favour.

2. It is, moreover, a character which *is generally well pleased with itself.* This feature is brought out very strikingly in the Epistle before us: "Thou sayest, I am rich, and increased with goods, and have need of nothing." It is a very natural accompaniment of such a character, and proceeds in a measure from the same causes which conciliate for it the favour of the world. When men have a high standard of life—a lofty ideal to which they feel bound to conform them-

selves—they feel the need of earnest effort in order to attain to it, and they are sure to meet with many disappointments on the way. It is, of course, otherwise with the lukewarm. With them there is little effort, and therefore a very slight realisation of the struggle which is involved in pressing on to the work which is set before us. They compare themselves, not with something which is far above them, but with themselves and with their neighbours, especially with those whom they consider worse than themselves. The natural result is an increased self-complacency. We see it in the Pharisee of our Lord's parable. The poor Publican, who could only beat upon his breast and utter the humble cry for mercy, went down to his house justified rather than the other. And yet that other formed a totally different judgement of their state before the Most High: "God, I thank Thee that I am not as other men are, or even as this Publican." It is the same with the Church of Laodicea: "Thou sayest, I am rich, and increased with goods, and have need of nothing." Self-righteousness is the almost inseparable characteristic of lukewarmness.

3. This is man's judgement of the character. It is more important that we should know *what Christ thinks of it*, if we are to decide how we as Christians must regard it. And He tells us His estimate, in language clear and strong and terrible to think of. We have read it. Let us meditate upon it.

Does it not sound almost more like the language of human impatience than of Divine love? Nothing is more insipid or distasteful than lukewarm food or drink. We can eat and drink that which is hot, and that which is cold; but we find the tepid or lukewarm sickening. We apply the comparison to men who are neither warm friends nor pronounced enemies. You know what to do with an enemy. You have to guard against him, and take care that he does not do you an injury. You know how to think of a true and constant friend. He is to be trusted in your presence, or in your absence. But a lukewarm friend —you never know what to do with him. He is ardently with you in prosperity; and in adversity he falls away from you, even when he does not turn against you. When all men speak well of you his voice joins readily and lustily to swell the chorus; but when the tide turns against you, he has not a word to say in your defence. Such people are not so uncommon in the world as we might wish; and perhaps most of us have had experience of them. We have used language respecting them not unlike the words of this epistle: "I would thou wert cold or hot!"

Such language, one feels, is very natural, and perhaps not very culpable, in the lips of men: is it worthy of the Son of God? We must carefully examine it It was certainly employed by our blessed Lord; and if there are seeming difficulties connected with it, that is the greater reason for studying it closely.

One thing we are quite sure it does not mean. It does not mean that weak grace is worse than no grace. Our Lord rejoices to see the faint and feeble beginning of the life of faith, never checks or discourages it, but adds strength and energy to it by every means. The bruised reed He will not break; the smoking flax He will not quench.

We shall understand who the lukewarm is when

we consider who are the cold and the hot. The hot are those who have a true and fervent love for God. The cold are those who have never truly experienced the grace of Christ. The lukewarm is one with whom the Gospel has failed. He has become hot, perhaps, but has immediately lost the fervour of love; or he has never advanced further from the state of coldness than to lukewarmness. He has "tasted of the heavenly gift," but he has abandoned it and turned away from it. The three classes come out in the ministry of our Lord: the Disciples are the hot, the Publicans and Harlots are the cold, the Scribes and Pharisees are the lukewarm.* In one sense the cold are worse than the lukewarm; but they are more hopeful.

We may now better understand the awful words which are spoken by Christ; and the more shall we be impressed by their truth, the more closely we consider the foundation on which they rest. The lukewarm are the most offensive to Him, for various reasons:

1. Such a character is *more dishonouring to God than either of the other two.* The lukewarm are taken as representatives of the spirit and life of the family of God. This, then, it is thought, is all that the grace of Christ can do. This is the effect of the work of redemption. This is the return which the loved ones of God make for the love with which He has loved them. We love Him, they say, because He first loved us; and this is the proof of it. The cold cannot dishonour God in this way. They do Him great wrong; but at least they are His enemies in name and position. In the other case "Wisdom is wounded in the house of her friends."

* Archbishop Trench.

2. Such a character is also *most hurtful to others.* The cold, the sinner, the ungodly, the mere man of the world—these characters are mischievous enough. But we know them for what they are. Their example is pernicious, and their influence is destructive; but the snare is spread in the sight of the bird, and he sees it while he suffers himself to be entangled in it. It is quite otherwise with the evil and pestilential influence of the lukewarm. They profess to be Christians, and they pass for Christians—sometimes for the best of that class; and they do deadly injury to the unwary who see their manner of life. In some they create a profound dislike for the Gospel itself; in others they produce the impression that a man may be a Christian without even trying to be like Christ.

It must needs be so with the untaught and inexperienced. One man says: Why should I be a Christian? It is a mere farce to take that name and remain the same as I was before. I am as good a man now as I should be then; nay, better, for then I should be just as bad, and a hypocrite into the bargain. With another the effect is different. He perhaps had serious thoughts of being a Christian, because he felt sure, in some vague kind of way, that there were advantages connected with it. Christianity, he may say, is the religion of the country; it is professed in some fashion by all my friends, neighbours, acquaintances. Nay, more, I am assured that men die more peacefully and more hopefully for being Christians. Perhaps, if I am one, it may be better for me in the next world. And then I can be a Christian without in any way changing my manner of life; for my friend is exactly the same as I am in principles, in sentiments, in life; and he considers himself an eminently consistent Christian, and is so regarded by the world around him. My brethren, let us look well at this; let us earnestly consider it. This is a kind of injury which cannot be inflicted on his fellow man by the hot or the cold. This mischief can be done only by the lukewarm.

3. But, once more on this point: it is a character which is *most dangerous to itself*. It offers an obstacle to the communication and reception of Divine grace, which neither of the other states can present. It has no consciousness of need, and therefore no longing for the supply which God in His mercy has provided. It is obviously the most difficult of all characters to alarm and arouse. The thunders of the law cannot arouse it from its sense of security. The fire of heavenly love which issues from the Gospel message does not melt its rocky self-complacency. Our blessed Lord told the lukewarm religionists of His day—"The Publicans and Harlots go into the Kingdom of Heaven before you."

And, then, it is a character which ever goes from bad to worse, which quenches more and more the good Spirit of God, and falls increasingly under the power of evil. There is but one end for it. It is that which is announced with such awful solemnity by our Lord: "So then because thou art lukewarm, and neither cold nor hot, I will spue thee out of my mouth." It is a threat of utter rejection and destruction, and of rejection with the most intense disgust. My brethren, our question was: What are we to think of this character? And we have seen what the world thinks of it, what it thinks of itself, and what our Lord thinks of it. Let us concentrate our attention, for the present, on one point. What shall we think of it, if perchance it is to be found in ourselves? Are you of those who are neither cold nor hot? Am I among the lukewarm? What a fearful possibility does such a question suggest! What an inward horror and fear should be aroused within us lest our Lord should so judge of us, and so judging should of us speak that terrible sentence of reprobation!

III. We seem almost to stand in doubt as to whether we have a right to advance to the third question. *How are we to deal with this character?* It may seem as though the considerations to which we have just referred forbade our entertaining such a question. A character like this, of which such things are said by Christ, must surely be hopeless. It is very nearly so, we must admit—more nearly so than, perhaps, any other character that we can readily think of; at least, I do not know another of which such awful words are spoken. But it is not absolutely hopeless, because we have no right to say that of any character but one; and, moreover, at the very moment that our Lord utters His terrible threat, He adds words which prove that the sentence is not irreversible—that there is still hope even for the lukewarm. Even they may be dealt with, for Christ actually counsels them what they are to do, and sets before them a promise in case they are victorious.

"I counsel thee," he says. "Wise as thou art, thou still needest my counsel; and I, slighted as I have been, give it freely." And what is His advice? "Buy of Me gold tried in the fire, that thou mayest be rich; and white raiment that thou mayest be clothed, and that the shame of thy nakedness do not appear; and anoint thine eyes with eye-salve, that thou mayest see." The words which He adds are words of wonderful tenderness. "As many as I love, I rebuke and chasten." I still love thee, in spite of all thy unfaithfulness, in spite of the disgust with which I regard thy sin. "Be zealous, therefore, and repent;" for the way of repentance is still open to thee, and thou mayest tread it.

1. The lukewarm are directed to Christ. "Buy of Me." It was through turning from Him that they had fallen: it is only by coming back to Him that they can rise again. Jesus Christ alone can give the remedy for the evils of sin and unbelief, and He has it and can give it.

2. But He further tells them what they are to seek for—"eye-salve, that" they "may see." It is the last mentioned, but it is the first thing needed. Perhaps there is not one of us who does not need to ask for this gift of Christ. We may not be so miserably blind as this lukewarm character which says it is rich, and knows nothing of its own poverty and blindness. But we are all of us afflicted in some measure with a blindness to our own faults and frailties. And only the eye-salve which Christ can give to anoint our eyes with has power to restore to us the spiritual vision which we have lost; only the light of the Holy Spirit, promised to lead us into all truth, to convince men of sin, of righteousness, and of judgment, can drive away the darkness of nature and the thick darkness of self-esteem and self-righteousness.

Then they are to buy gold, the gold of faith, which alone is the true riches of the Christian, and which they had exchanged for the pinchbeck of prudence and worldly wisdom; and the white raiment of righteousness, of justification and sanctification, the white robe of Christ, which covers the nakedness of our fallen state; and the wedding garment, wrought in us and on us by the Holy Spirit of God, that we may be prepared to sit down at the wedding supper of the Lamb. What is the meaning of it all but this? We must restore our Lord Jesus Christ to His rightful place of supremacy in our heart and life; and we must seek for, and depend upon, the grace of His Holy Spirit, to turn us more and more to Him, and to transform us into His likeness.

3. And all this He says we are to *buy*. Let us mark the word. It needs and demands consideration. The grace of God is free. We could not merit it or gain it in any way, and yet our Lord says we are to *buy* of Him. It is not here alone that this seeming contradiction appears. The prophet Isaiah summons all who thirst to come to the waters, and he bids them come and buy wine and milk "without money and without price." It is quite clear that we can give to Almighty God and to our Blessed Lord no equivalent for the good things with which we are supplied by Divine grace. "Nothing in my hand I bring" is the sentiment expressed or implied in every humble and trustful approach to the throne of grace.

And yet we are to *buy*. What does it mean? It means, it must mean—there is, in fact, no other meaning imaginable under the circumstances—that we must part with something in order to appropriate these blessings to ourselves. They must cost us something, although we can give God nothing, certainly not a fair equivalent, for what He gives us. And what must we part with? We must part with our *self-righteousness.* We must abandon our flattering opinions of ourselves. We must become emptied of self, poor in spirit, humble, and contrite. We must learn from our heart to say with S. Paul, "What things were gain to me, those I counted loss for Christ. Yea, doubtless, and I count all things but loss, for the excellency of the knowledge of Christ Jesus my Lord, for whom I have suffered the loss of all things, and do count them but dung, that I may win Christ, and be found in Him, not having mine own righteousness, which is of the law, but that which is through the faith of Christ, the righteousness which is of God by faith."

We must part with our *sloth and self-will.* The Christian life, to be a reality, must be a sacrifice from beginning to end. The ways of wisdom are "ways of pleasantness, and all her paths are peace." The "yoke" of Christ "is easy;" His "burden is light." And yet we can truly come after Him only as we deny ourselves, and take up our cross and follow Him. We must crucify the world and the flesh. The *sloth,* which would bid us defer or omit the accustomed hour of prayer, must be sacrificed. The *self-indulgence,* which would bid us make light of the duties which, as faithful servants, we owe to our Master, must be sacrificed. We must have no ruler and no law of life but Jesus Christ, His example, and His Holy Spirit. This is the price we must pay; and although, when we have done all, we must confess ourselves unprofitable servants, yet He will not refuse to accept it.

My brethren, it is a very solemn subject on which I have endeavoured to speak to you. I have been trying to produce in you the same disgust for this horrid vice of lukewarmness which is entertained for it by our Lord. I have meant to induce you to strive against it with all your might by the power of the Spirit of Christ Jesus. It is a fearful evil: an indignity to the God of Love, a fruitful source of evil to the Church and to the world, a plague-spot in the life of him who is infected with it. It is the enemy of God and of man. Christ is seeking to bring the charge home to us this night. "Behold," he says, "I stand at the door and knock." Are we keeping Him out, or are we opening and letting Him in? Let none of us say that he is not one of the lukewarm. Let us examine ourselves in the light of God, and if we find in ourselves this evil thing, let us lay it before Him for destruction; let us open wide the door of our hearts, that He may enter in, and take whole and undisputed possession of them; for thus alone shall no place be found for this accursed thing within us.

IX.

OUR DIVISIONS,

BY THE

REV. M. F. SADLER, M.A.,

Prebendary of Wells, and Rector of Honiton.

Our Divisions.

EPHESIANS iv., 4.

"One body, and one spirit"

DIVISIONS: whence come they? whither tend they—to good or to evil?

If we had only the New Testament, and no history of the Church from the time of the Apostles to the present, there would be little difficulty about these questions; for the Lord Himself is one with the Father and the Holy Ghost in the highest and most perfect of all unities—the unity of the Trinity; and He came to make His people one, for He came to gather together into one the children of God which were scattered abroad. If we are to judge of what were the cravings of His heart from that wondrous unbosoming of all that is in His soul to His Father, which He poured forth on the way to Gethsemane, then the oneness of His Church was "the thing that He longed for." "Holy Father," He prays, "keep through Thine own name those whom Thou hast given Me, that they may be one, as we are. Neither pray I for these alone, but for them also which shall believe on Me through their word; that they all may be one, as Thou, O Father, art in Me, and I in Thee;

that they also may be one in us, that the world may believe that Thou hast sent Me." And again: "I in them, and Thou in Me; that they may be made perfect in one, that the world may believe that Thou hast sent Me." See, I beseech you, how earnestly He pleads for unity.

Then the sacrifice He offered was a sacrifice of reconciliation, not only to bring about reconciliation between God and man, but between man and his fellow-man. As His great servant and Apostle tells us, "He gave Himself, that He might reconcile both —*i.e.*, the two divisions of mankind—unto God in one body by the Cross, having slain the enmity thereby. (Ephesians ii., 16.)

The prayer which He taught is a prayer of unity— "OUR Father—forgive us OUR trespasses, as we forgive them that trespass against us."

The Sacraments He instituted are sacraments of unity. In the one, "by One Spirit we are all baptised into one body." In the other, "we, being many, are one bread and one body; for we are all partakers of that one bread." (1 Cor, xii., 13; and x., 17.) The Church He instituted is one in the sense of being one organisation. "There is one body;" not only one spirit, one faith, one hope, one baptism, but one body; and this not as a matter of mere dogma, or of speculation, but as a practical matter, which, if a man realised, he would, in the eyes of the Apostle, be in the way of being a better Christian. For instance, the Apostle writes, "I beseech you that ye walk worthy of the vocation wherewith ye are called, with all lowliness and meekness, with long-suffering, forbearing one another in love, endeavouring to keep the unity of the spirit in the bond of peace; for there is one body and one spirit." Here it would seem that the Apostle reminds the Christian that one body cannot have two spirits, just as two bodies (in the sense of two organisations) cannot have one spirit; so that if a Christian would endeavour to keep the unity of the spirit, he can only do it by realising the unity of the organisation of which Christ is the Head.

This is the positive doctrine which, beyond all contradiction, is set forth in the New Testament; and there is a counterpart doctrine in all respects answering to it, which is this—that any divisions whatsoever, whether in the shape of a schism creating a new external body or in the shape of a party or school existing in the one body, are not from God, but "come of evil."

First of all, consider that among the works of the flesh, which you heard enumerated in the Epistle for the first day of this very week, we have "hatred, variance, wrath, strife, sedition, heresies, envyings." (Gal. v., 20.)

Then remember that the Apostle writes to a Church in which divisions were rife in such terms as these—"Ye are yet carnal; for whereas there is among you envyings, strife, and divisions, are ye not carnal? For while one says, I am of Paul; and another, I am of Apollos; are ye not carnal?" (1 Cor., iii., 4.)

But it may be said—Were not men then as they are now? Have they not differently-constituted minds, and so must they not, of necessity, take different views of Divine truth? Now, whatever truth there is in this objection (and that there is much truth in it I shall presently show), the Apostle, in the case of his Corinthian converts, ignores it as irrelevant, and lays down a law of unity in speech and thought as absolute as can well be conceived.

"Now I beseech you, brethren, in the name of our Lord Jesus Christ, that ye all speak the same thing, and that there be no divisions among you, but that ye be perfectly joined together in the same mind and in the same judgment." Such is the utterance of this greatest of merely human teachers; such is, rather, the utterance of that Spirit of God—that Spirit of unity, sevenfold in His actings, but one in His Divine essence, Who spake by the Apostle.

I have now given what, I think, all must acknowledge to be the view of this matter contained in the New Testament. There is nothing that I can remember contrary to this; nothing that I can remember which even modifies or relaxes it. I do not for a moment deny—indeed, I wish to assert it—that there are indications of much freer action, especially in the matter of teaching; but the free action, if it be from God, is supposed to assist in the building-up of one body—not in the multiplication of bodies or Churches without the Church. And, of course, it is always assumed to teach the one faith once delivered to the saints; so that all may come in the unity of that faith and of the knowledge of the Son of God, to a perfect man.

Such, I repeat, is the teaching of the New Testament.

How are we now to apply it? Are we to say that our Church alone, even though it has the most indubitable marks of the one body or organisation, is the Church, and our way of thinking alone is the truth? Must we protest vehemently, must we rebuke with sharpness, must we call upon all at once to conform to our view, both outwardly and in the spirit.

My brethren, the Church has not only a book to direct it; it has a history—a history in which it has been guided by a special Providence, which history it is impossible to ignore in any *bona-fide* attempt which we may make to ascertain the will of God.

Now the first thing which strikes us in this history is the declension from its original purity, and fervour, and love, of *the* body, which, if there be any such thing as a visible Church at all, is entitled from its history and from its genealogy, so to speak, to be called the Church. Take what was undoubtedly the Church in Western Europe at the time of the Reformation. What was *the* cause of that division—the precedent, be it remembered, and justification of every other division since then? Not dogma, not transubstantiation, not even want of definite views on justification, but shameless corruption. The Sovereign Pontiff who drove Luther into what is called schism was an infidel; his court—at least that of some of his immediate predecessors—the most shameless in Europe; archbishoprics were given to boys, the very priests at the altar not believing, in any sense, the very words of institution.

One who assuredly *has* not (and never had) the smallest leaning to Lutheranism has written—"In behalf of the Foreign Communities it may be pleaded that they were excluded by unjust excommunication, and that their exclusion was perpetuated by an iron necessity, galling their conscience to the very quick."* But, you may rejoin, we have to speak

* Manning on the Unity of the Church, page 344.

about *our* divisions; and all this was nigh four hundred years ago. Yes; but this was the letting out of the waters. This was the time of the assertion, not merely of private judgment, but of the right of any person who chose to form an organisation independent of, or antagonistic to, the one Christian organisation then existing.

And now let us look at home. Let us take the Church of seventy or a hundred years ago in this country. How did it fulfil the command of the Saviour, "Feed my sheep?" The sheep of Christ have to be fed both with doctrine and Eucharist. The doctrine with which they have to be fed is the doctrine of His Body—how God became Incarnate, took a Body, was made flesh, gave that Body in sacrifice, rose again in that Body in token of the acceptance of the sacrifice, ascended in that Body into Heaven, made that blessed natural Body the root of a mystical Body, so identified with Himself that He is in them, and they in Him. This is the truth which the sheep of Christ have to be fed with, that they may grow up in Christ.

But along with this mental feeding—this appeal to the faith of the heart and spirit—there is also a sacramental feeding never to be disjoined from it; nay, the sacramental feeding embodies the first truths of the other, so that if we would eat "discerning the Lord's body" we must realise Church crucified in the heart. Well, now, how did the Church of Christ in this country, at the time I allude to, feed the flock of Christ? Why, if the truth respecting the person and work of Christ be the food of the Christian's soul, she starved them. If the Eucharist be the means whereby we feed on the flesh of the Son of Man, she fed them four times a-year; and very, very often, not that.

But, you will say, was there not then the Liturgy? Yes, there was not only the Liturgy, but the Bible. But the Liturgy, as well as the Bible, has to be taught, has to be worked, has to be lived; and, however perfect the Church may be on paper, the priest of each parish is the agent through whom she acts, through whom the people know her; without whom, in fact, she is, to all intents and purposes, a dead letter.

Well, as we all know—as we have been reminded times without number—as we have, perhaps, some of us reminded others times without number—there was a stirring-up of the religious heart of the people both within and without the Church. The stirring, both within and without, was of the same character, of the same pattern or type. It was a stirring-up of men's minds and hearts to embrace the truth that each one who has the use of his faculties must for himself come to Christ, believe in Christ, accept Christ, be washed in the blood of Christ, mentally or spiritually feed on Christ, and at the last be found in Christ.

Those in the Church who thus had their eyes opened to the most precious truths of the Gospel naturally found one another out, held together, encouraged one another, took means to spread the knowledge of salvation, and so far as they were able, whilst within the Church, instituted organisations for the spread of the truth at home and abroad.

But there was an external movement also. The movements under Wesley and Whitfield, contrary to the wish and prayers of one at least of these, took a more independent course, and gradually became compact and well-organised bodies without the Church.

Other bodies, such as those popularly called the Irvingites and the Plymouth Brethren, sprung up at a later period, and are far more powerful from the talent, influence, position, wealth, and earnestness of their members than their numbers would lead us to expect.

A town in which till very lately I was a minister may be taken as a type of the results of all this.

This town contained six Churches. The ministers of some of these, though living on the most Christian terms, and also having, I may testify, a strong personal friendship for one another, never exchanged pulpits. Among those external to the Church of England there were three Episcopal bodies—Roman Catholic, Irvingite, Moravian. There was a meeting-house, which was originally the one in which the greatest name in Nonconformity once ministered, which was composed of Baptists and Independents; and there was another, of Independents only. There were four Baptist places of worship, three out of the four not holding communion with one another; and during the few years of my residence there the small band of the "Brethren," as they were called, was divided, the one part ceasing to hold communion with the other.

I suppose that this is not an exaggerated type, in the matter of religious division, of most English or American towns. You will understand, I trust, that I am not, in drawing attention to all this, trying to make out a case for our Church. On the contrary, for the first thing I drew attention to was the party divisions in that Church; and I may also mention that in by far the most populous and poorest parish of the town I allude to there were, twenty or thirty years ago, not fifty free seats in which the poor could come and worship God without the danger of being turned out into the aisles. In the memory of many living men two, if not more, of the older Churches were held by one person; and there had scarcely been ever known such a thing as a resident incumbent of the principal Church.

Such is our present state. East and West divided; and the principal Bishop of the West asserting his own infallibility, and making this and the Immaculate Conception terms of communion.

Protestants hopelessly divided; German Lutheranism more than half rationalistic; all the principal national Churches of the Continent Socinianised; Calvin's own pulpit occupied by men symbolising more with Servetus than with himself; and the state of England and America such as I have described by the case of one town.

Such is the state of things in which we live. Need it have been so? What is the effect of it all? What is our duty?

Need it have been so? You see I do not say, "Need it be so?" Past generations have sown. We are now reaping the harvest of which they have sown the seed. But *need* all this have been?

Now I desire you to remember the evidence I brought forward from the New Testament respecting the design of God and the desire of Christ that there should be one body, one organisation, one fellowship; and I ask you to look upon the fall of the Church from her first unity in the light of that well-known passage of God's word—"God is faithful, who will not suffer you to be tempted above that ye are able, but will with the temptation make a way to escape, that ye may be able to bear it." (1 Cor., x., 13.) We know that in the case of temptation to other breaches of God's law this will be found at the last great day to have been true in every case. Then God, when He confronts men with their sin, will bring to mind how in each case there was a way of escape; and they knew it, for it was open before them; and when they fell, it was because they turned themselves away from the deliverance God had set before them. And can we suppose for a moment that in this matter of unity, for which Christ prayed so earnestly, there has ever been a necessity laid upon men to divide the Church of Christ? No. Let us us believe that God is faithful in this, as in all else.

I could mention several facts in the history of great leaders of thought or religion in the Church, which show that in the most remarkable crises of their spiritual lives God so dealt with them that if they would have remembered His dealings they would have impressed quite another spirit on those who had followed them. Take, first of all, Simeon, the great leader of Evangelical religion in Cambridge. How, according to his biographer, was it that he found "peace with God?" In reading a book of the High Church Wilson, Bishop of Sodor and Man, on preparation for the Eucharist.

Again, how was J. H. Newman first led to see the truth of the first of all Church principles, the doctrine of grace in Baptism? From reading a work of the late Archbishop Sumner. How did Chalmers, a great party leader in the Kirk of Scotland, get his religion? From reading Wilberforce's "Practical View of Christianity."

Again: take two other facts. You all doubtless

remember well the great Advent Mission of two years ago in London. Consider the character of the preaching then resorted to—of a distinctly revival character, the most advanced Churchmen using extempore prayers in Church, and Bible classes in the vestry. And almost immediately after this there was a great meeting of the leading clergymen of the opposite school in Islington, at which a Canon of your own Cathedral of Wells begged his Evangelical brethren to consider whether, though they had abundantly called upon their hearers to make good each one for himself his individual interest in Christ, there had not been amongst them as a party an almost total ignoring of Christ as the Head of a Church, the Saviour of a Body—in fact, an almost total ignoring of the Church principle of the New Testament.

Again: within the last year or so certain hymns of Wesley have been reprinted, with the strongest approval of the party reprinting them, as being the very best hymns he is acquainted with for enabling those who use them to realise a great doctrinal truth. What doctrine do you suppose that to be? No other than the Sacrifice in the Eucharist. And who is the reprinter and recommender of these hymns? The Editor of the most advanced Ritualistic newspaper—the *Church Times*. Now take the significance of the first of these facts—the Rev. Charles Simeon obtaining a sense of peace from a book of Bishop Wilson's. Surely that was a message to him to give at least patient attention to other truths which that saintly Bishop taught! And, if he had done so, God knows how much nearer the two great parties of the Church would have now been to one another.

What is the effect of the divisions of the Church?

We have the terrible effect indicated in the prayer of our great Head.

He prays "that they all may be one, as Thou Father art in me, and I in Thee, that the world may believe that Thou hast sent Me." The Church has not been, as yet, one; and the world does not believe that God has sent Christ. At this very day, in this 1871st year of grace—think of that word "year of grace,"—year, that is, since the great fountain of grace has been opened in this world for its cleansing of life, in this very year of grace, I say, two-thirds (some say more) of the dwellers upon this redeemed earth do not believe that God sent Christ; and this because of the divisions of the Church.

But, it may be rejoined, have not the divisions of Christendom multiplied the organisations of Christendom for the conversion of the heathen?

Yes, but what, putting all together, have they done—I mean, of course, compared to the work to be done? What impression has been made upon the mass of Mahomedanism, the mass of Brahminism, the mass of Budhism? I say this remembering the work done among the simple impressible islanders of the South Seas, and among the negroes of West Africa and the West, and the noble work among the Malagasays in Madagascar, and the Karens of the Burman Empire. Here, then, I grant, I thankfully grant, that God has shown His power. But the great masses of heathenism seem untouched; and if the continued existence of heathenism abroad is due to our divisions, what must we say of heathenism at home—of the heathen masses of our large towns? Can we apply one rule or principle to account for the continued existence of old heathenism in India and China, and another to account for the new heathenism of London and Birmingham and New York?

When God first, on the Day of Pentecost, rained down the spirit and founded the Church, to what had He listened? To the continuous united prayer of the then united Church; and it may be He waits for the same now.

The Apostle St. Peter writes to his converts a sentence which seems to be wonderfully suggestive of the effect of our divisions. "Give honour," he says to husbands; "give honour to the wife, as the weaker vessel, and as being heirs together of the grace of life; that your prayers be not hindered."

If divisions in a family hinder prayers and restrain blessings, so must divisions in a parish, in a diocese, in the national church, in the Church of God.

And surely you must have experienced, brethren—at least I have,—how distracting to devotion is a controversial frame — how Satan amuses us and draws off our minds in public prayer, even at the Eucharist, by trains of controversial thought, which perhaps a word in the very service suggests, but which trains of thought we must at once put out of our minds, if we would lift up our hearts to God, as we would put out a worldly or an unclean thought.

And now, brethren, what is our duty? Our duty is not to compromise the truth, or to withhold the truth, or to water down the truth which God, we believe, has shown to us; but our duty is to remember that truth is many-sided, and that a man may hold the very truth which we do, and yet not express it in the same way. Let us also remember that one aspect of the truth lays hold of one mind, and another of another. Look at the college of the Apostles. There can be no doubt that there are three modes of expressing Divine truth in the very New Testament itself, viz., those adopted by St. Paul, St. John, and St. James respectively.

Again: let us glorify God whenever we see or read of the fruits of faith, even in those who differ most widely from us.

We can do this in almost every case without compromising our own principles.

I suppose no Christian can withhold his thanks to God when he reads of the martyrdom of Romish missionaries in the 17th century in Japan, or in this century in Cochin China; just as he must thank God for the faithfulness unto death of those converted to Christ by Congregational missionaries in Madagascar.

And surely we can avow our convictions that these were genuine fruits of faith without being supposed, on the one hand, to lean towards the Immaculate Conception of the Virgin; or, on the other, to the opinion that Christ has left no organisation in His Church except the organisation of the separate and ever separating congregation.

But, lastly, let us for our own souls' sake remember that before we can think of, much less pray for, unity, our souls must be in union with God. Unity, as well as charity, must begin at home. First of all, our own souls must be reconciled to God, must partake of the atonement, must be united to Him through his Son by His Spirit; and then our souls must be at peace with our neighbours and brethren; and then, and not till then, can we pray for, hope for, work for, unity in the Church of God.

X.

SLOTH,

BY THE

REV. E. H. PLUMPTRE, M.A.,

PROFESSOR OF DIVINITY IN KING'S COLLEGE, LONDON;

PREBENDARY OF S. PAUL'S, AND RECTOR OF PLUCKLEY, KENT.

Sloth.

PROV. xxiv., 30, 31, 32.

"I went by the field of the slothful, and by the vineyard of the man void of understanding, and lo! it was all grown over with thorns, and nettles had covered the face thereof, and the stone wall thereof was broken down. Then I saw, and considered it well; I looked upon it, and received instruction."

YOU will observe that in this, as in other instances, the Proverbs take chiefly the starting-point of prudence. They dwell on sin so far as it is folly—on its consequences as affecting a man's fortune or reputation. They speak of sloth, wrath, hastiness, as mistakes—blunders in life—the extreme of secular, as well as spiritual, unwisdom. This was natural enough, in harmony with the general character of proverbial instruction. Proverbs always do address themselves to the broad, popular, common-sense judgment of the intellect. They may rest on the ground-work of a deep, universal truth, as those of Scripture for the most part do; but they do not bring it prominently forward. They may admit of manifold applications to the higher life of man; but the immediate range of application is, for the most part, limited to the common work and circumstances of his lower life, and meant to guide him safely through them.

This was the measure of truth given to the writers of the Proverbs of Israel. There is no irreverence in saying that it was not the same measure as that which was revealed to Prophets whose eyes had seen the King, the Lord of Hosts—to Apostles to whom it was given to know the mysteries of the Kingdom of Heaven. Every day's experience shows us, indeed, that such teaching can never become obsolete—can never safely be dispensed with. We need it because we have not yet attained to the higher knowledge, and are slowly climbing up the hill of truth, and require the discipline of prudence to prepare us for the capacity of faith. Here also the law holds good, that "first cometh that which is natural, and afterwards that which is spiritual." Or we need it because that knowledge has been given to us, and there is danger lest, while we look upwards and gaze on its exceeding brightness, we may fall unawares into some of the traps and pitfalls which still lie round our path. It is simply the blindness of unwisdom for the most advanced and illuminated disciple to think that he is above the rules of prudence and the current judgments of mankind. Proverbs, inspired or uninspired, are often wholesome checks on the self-deception of the dreamer, or the pride of the formalist. Prudence in earthly things is a condition—not, of course, the only one—of forethought in spiritual, just as honesty in the workshop or the market-place is a condition of the blessedness of the upright and the pure in heart. "If ye have not been faithful in the unrighteous mammon, who will commit to your charge the true riches. And if ye have not been faithful in that which is another man's, who shall give you that which is your own."

But he is a poor student of proverbs and parables who does not see that in well-nigh all cases they branch out into manifold applications, and go deeper down into the root and ground of things than at first sight appeared. All things are double one against another. The natural world is the parable of the simply human—the human of the spiritual. Each comparison, drawn from either, has many points of affinity with the other two. In those old forms of speech which belong to the universal language of mankind, and have become so familiar to us that we have well nigh forgotten the boldness of the comparisons on which they rest—the keenness of insight implied in the perception of resemblances, where, at first sight, there seemed only differences—we may find examples by which the mind of man passes from one stage to another, and, as its own experience becomes higher, finds it possible to translate whatever is new, wonderful, transcendent, into the old and simple language.

In this parable of the sluggard there lie accordingly meanings that are below the surface. To every man who has become conscious of his humanity—to every Christian, therefore, who has been solemnly called to the knowledge of his glorious inheritance—there has been allotted a field, which he may make fruitful—a vineyard, which the Lord has planted. Like the first created man, he is set in the garden of the Lord to dress it and to keep it. In that garden of the soul, as in the Paradise of old, there is every tree that is pleasant to the sight and good for food—wide regions of beauty and fertility, able to fill the hungry soul with fatness and to refresh the weary. There also grow the tree of life and the tree of the knowledge of good and evil. We may understand the full wretchedness of the picture which the teaching of the wise man brings before us by comparing that scene of desolation with the beauty and brightness which, however seldom realised, are, at least, in their measure possible—which come in some degree as the reward of all honest and hearty effort to obtain them. We may think of the man as soon as he takes any cognisance of the work before him, devoting himself to it with a vigorous and stedfast will. The words of one who sought the Kingdom of God and His righteousness may be taken as the type and pattern of this blameless life—"When I was yet young, or ever I went abroad, I desired wisdom openly in my prayer. I prayed for her before the Temple, and will seek her out even unto the end. Even from the flower till the grape was ripe has my heart delighted in her. My foot went the right way: from my youth up sought I after her." (Ecclus. li., 13—15.) To such a man the culture of his own heart (what a whole world of parables, too, lies in that single phrase!) is no light or trivial matter. It is the task to which God has called him—to which his whole life must be devoted. It is in that field that the Sower, who is the Son of Man, has scattered freely that seed of the Word of God which may bring forth fruit unto life eternal. There the seed which has been so sown springs up: first the blade—the tender, weak beginnings of good thoughts and purposes of amendment; then the ear—the acts that give good promise of the future, and help in the development of character; after that the full corn in the ear—the ripened and completed holiness of the saints of God. There is the vineyard, which God has planted with the choicest vine, out of which, in the season of the vintage, comes the wine that maketh glad the heart of man—that blood of the grape which is worthy to be poured out as an acceptable offering unto the Most High, the King of all the earth. He who would be a faithful labourer in that vineyard—a fellow-worker in that husbandry of God—must be active, watchful, faithful; for there also the enemy comes and sows tares in the field, and plants the wild vines that bear but bitter fruit. There also the foxes spoil the tender vines. The boar out of the wood doth waste it, and the wild beast of the field doth devour it. And in this inward husbandry—this tillage of the soul—that is possible which the Great Lord of the harvest has declared to be impossible in the field which answers to the great heritage of the Church. No command has gone forth here bidding us to let both wheat and tares grow together unto the harvest. It is the work of every man to anticipate so far as he is able the final sentence—to judge himself that he be not judged of the Lord, and to root out from his soul every plant of which he is sure that it is of evil, and not of good, and that, therefore, his Heavenly Father has not planted it.

And here, too, that is the very law of growth which, in the world of Nature, is a rare and marvellous exception. Here the prayer, not only of the righteous man, but of the humblest seeker after righteousness, availeth much, and the rain of heaven falls in answer to it; and so the fields are clothed with their springtide apparel, and "the Spirit is poured from on high, and the wilderness becomes a fruitful field, and the fruitful field is counted as a forest." The endeavour of the true husbandman is to draw upon that field of his the abundant, life-giving showers of the grace of God. He seeks that through it his heart may never be hard like the wayside soil, that the ground may be deep and rich. He guards against the growth of the thorns which, even in the most fruitful soil, may spring up and choke the seed of the Word of Life, so that it becomes unfruitful. And he who has taken a true measure of the extent and nature of the work before him—who has, as it were, surveyed the field which is given him as an heritage—will know that each region of it has its own special growth, and that none must be neglected. The soul of the wise of heart is like the garden of Solomon, which the Song of Songs brings before us in all its loveliness. There the flowers appear upon the earth, and the fig-tree putteth forth her green figs, and the tender grape appears, and the pomegranates bud forth; and at the gates are all manner of pleasant fruits, new and old, which he has laid up—even the Lord—for his beloved. Knowledge, and wisdom, and strength, and courage, and purity, and truth, and meekness, and kindness, largeness of heart and intensity of love, reverence for the past and hope for the future, the sympathy which shuts out none from fellowship, the firmness which continues stedfast and immovable against evil—all these we may picture to ourselves as the elements of the perfect character; all these are found in the soul which, watered by the continual due of God's blessing, has become fair and fruitful as the Paradise of God. But that this may be the result there must be care, activity, discernment. "I went by the field of the slothful, and by the vineyard of the man void of understanding; and lo! it was all grown over with thorns, and nettles had covered the face thereof, and the stone wall thereof was broken down." There, in that neglected garden of the heart and spirit of man, all is disorder, unsightliness, decay. "Things rank and gross in nature possess it merely." The elements of good which belonged to the natural character have spread out beyond their proper bounds, and so have lost their beauty and are no longer fruitful. The vine, which God had planted wholly right, has become "as the degenerate plant of the wild vine," and its clusters are few, and the wine that is pressed from them is harsh and sour. Thorns (we know at once how to interpret these), the cares of this life, and the deceitfulness of riches—the low aims and miserable anxieties which mix themselves with secular activity, but are just as liable to take root and grow in secular indolence and neglect—these are there, choking the good seed, rendering it altogether unfruitful. But negligence has yet worse results—"Nettles had covered the face thereof." Where there is no watchfulness, no activity in good, evil grows unbidden and diffuses itself with a terrible rapidity—sins against love, and purity, and truth; the rankest outgrowths of the lowest elements of our nature—these take possession of the soul. Unbelief, scorn, malignity—these are the unsightly, harmful products of the heritage, which might have been beautiful and fragrant as a field which the Lord has blessed.

Yes; and, to complete the scene of waste and utter desolation, "the stone wall thereof was broken down." That also was an essential condition of the husbandry. Without that there could be no security, no fruitfulness. It must strike every reader of the parables of Scripture, that in all which have the idea of the vineyard for their ground-work a very prominent position is assigned to that which is a simply defensive barrier. "My well-beloved hath a vineyard in a very fruitful hill, and he fenced it—made a wall about it." (Isaiah v., 2.) "There was a certain householder which planted a vineyard and hedged it round about." (Matt. 21, 33.) Must we not believe that this also has a meaning? Does it not point to a truth of immense importance in its bearings upon the spiritual life, upon all self-culture, upon all national and individual training? What is needed for the perfect growth of goodness is not merely the capacity for receiving good which answers to the fertile soil; nor the desire and purposes of good, which are to us the seed of eternal life, planted by the Heavenly sower; nor the help and strength of the grace of God's Holy Spirit, which is as the soft dew from Heaven. There must be also the defence of an outward discipline—the restraints of a rule which keeps us shut in from the attacks of the more hateful and deadly sins, which do their work of destruction rapidly. The discipline may seem simply formal; the restraints arbitrary and conventional. They are powerless to give life. The fence may encircle a barren as well as a fruitful vineyard; and yet we cannot spare it—are not safe without it. To the Jews as a nation the ordinances and customs which kept them a separate people, which made them in spite of themselves a witness against themselves, and were designed to hinder their adoption of the dark rites and hateful vices of the heathen, were for them the fence of the vineyard. The Church of Christ has in different ages had its fence of an established ritual — laws of discipline, fixed observances, the recurrence of holy seasons. Every society of men, aiming in ever so low a degree at the establishment of righteousness and truth, recognises the same necessity. You find it, I need hardly say, in the rules of every school and college. The conventional decencies which are to be found in all companionship but that of the most depraved have essentially the same character. That which makes the representation of the vineyard of the slothful so utterly dreary and hopeless is that this also is broken down. Indolence has passed into utter recklessness. It is an evil thing for a man to care only for the outward forms which guard the well-being of the Church, or of society, or of his own soul. It is still more evil and more perilous for him to become indifferent to them—to think that he may disregard them safely. Thus it is that first the foxes, and then the wild boar out of the wood, and the beast of the field, complete their work of devastation. There may be barrenness, and thorns, and nettles within the barrier; but remove the fence, and a thousand evils rush in which otherwise might have been kept off.

> Small sins the heart first desecrate;
> At last despair persuades to great.

The sight of that utter waste—of that transformation of the garden of the Lord into a howling wilderness—the spectacle of a soul over which the Tempter seems to have triumphed so completely, and evil to be altogether dominant—cannot but be a very sad and awful one. It fills us with many questions, many fears. In what did all this originate? Could this have been foreseen as it actually is, and then chosen in preference to the peace and blessedness of a life acceptable to God? Those questionings also have their counterpart in the parable—"Then I saw, and considered it well; I looked upon it, and received instruction." And the answer to them is found in the well-known, familiar words with which the chapter closes—"Yet a little sleep, a little slumber, a little folding of the hands to sleep. So shall thy poverty come as one that travelleth, and thy want as an armed one." There was, to start with, no intention to forfeit the inheritance of God's Kingdom and waste all gifts so utterly—no wish to be the object of wonder and pity to the good, of scorn or malignant satisfaction to the bad. There was no foresight of the middle life of shifts, and dishonour, and loss of self-respect—of the old age bankrupt in health, and purse, and character, and hope. In all the steps of this miserable descent the man sees but a little way before him. The idler, the shuffler, the equivocator with himself or others, is blind to what others discern clearly, that the course on which he has entered must end, here or elsewhere, in failure and disgrace. The man of weak, unstable character, who has no power to keep his ground, to say "No" firmly and persistently when tempted to run with others to their excess of riot, does not see that the drunkard's revelry must end in the drunkard's madness. He who yields to temptations of another kind would shudder, did he see himself, as he may one day be, at no remote future, the betrayer and the destroyer of innocence, the convicted and branded adulterer. In all these cases the evils to which a man has once consented gains upon him with a terrible rapidity. It is at first only sloth, and delay, and procrastination. He cannot rouse himself from the indolence which makes all efforts painful. Whatever restlessness there may be in outward things—whatever seeming activity for a time, though that in most cases soon disappears, there is no real energy of will, no watchfulness and diligence in the soul. Its eyes are closed. It dreams away its life, and takes its visions for realities. It folds its hands to slumber, not saying to itself that it will never wake, only asking for a little more sleep, a little more folding of the hands.

As regards our own spiritual life, the culture of our own souls, the lesson is very simple and obvious. "Awake thou that sleepest, and arise from the dead, and Christ shall give thee light." Now it is high time to awake out of sleep; the night is far spent, the day is at hand. "Be not slothful in your pursuit of good; be fervent in spirit, serving the Lord." Resolve from the first dawnings of a conscious power to choose between good and evil—that you will do the work to which God has called you faithfully; that you will do the tasks of each day in singleness of heart; that you will maintain, unbroken, the barriers of discipline and order which here or elsewhere are set up in the human or Divine society of which you are members, for your protection. Suffer not the thorns to grow up in their thick and rank luxuriance; grasp the nettles with a firm hand, and root them out; seek for and welcome the dew of God's grace; and then the Lord of the vineyard, the beloved of thy soul, shall in due time come into thy garden and eat its pleasant fruits. After the season of toil, endurance, faithfulness, there shall come the rich reward, and the gleaning of the grapes in that autumn of the soul shall be better than the whole vintage of those who labour for the rewards of earth.

All that I have said, brethren, admits of another

and a wider application. The parable is but half interpreted. I may not venture now on the region where its lessons are of greatest moment, in which the types find their most adequate fulfilment. The vineyard of the Lord of Hosts is the House of Israel, and the men of Judah his pleasant plant. It is into that vineyard—into the Church of God—that its Lord calls us to be labourers. Some portion of that is given to us all, that we may dress it and keep it. Thither also will the Lord come that He may receive the fruits thereof. There, too, are the same duties, risks, responsibilities. Here, also, there are the thorns, and the nettles, and the broken wall—the same scene of shame, and loss, and dishonour, in the field of the slothful and the vineyard of the man void of understanding. The history of the Church of Christ—your own experience, which, small as it may be, is a fragment of that great history—present manifold examples of the fruits of inactivity, blindness, procrastination. Do not let the lessons of the past be lost upon you. Now, if ever, do we need the spirit of prompt, persevering energy. Vast problems lie before us, and with them the opening of immense possibilities for good. The question whether the Church of England can re-model her services, her organisation, her discipline, so as to meet the wants of the age in which we live, and profit by the experience of her past failures; whether she can remove the stumbling-blocks of the *debris* of past controversies, and take her place once again as the leader of the religious life of the English nation; whether she is to retain any hold on the education of the people; whether she can help the State in its work, or must fall into a profitless antagonism, or an idle querulousness; all these are brought before us by the pressing exigencies of the hour. It is worse than fruitless, it is a blunder as well as a crime, to shrink from facing them. These cries of "The Church in danger;" the panic dread of change; the over-caution which leads to a policy of *laissez-faire*, which strives to keep everything in ritual or teaching as it is—that would fain fold its hands once more, and for ever, in the tranquil slumber of self-satisfied repose—this resistance to the counsels of wise and faithful reformers; what is this but to reproduce the sluggard of the Proverbs, who says that "there it a lion in the way—a lion is in the street;" who, when he is roused from sleep, turns upon his bed as "a door turneth upon its hinges;" who "is wiser in his own conceit than seven men that can render a reason." (Prov. xxvi., 13—16.) For us there is reserved, let us hope, a better and a nobler future. Whatever signs of decay there may have been in the past; whatever perils there may be in the present; there is no lack of energy and zeal. If that energy be rightly directed—if the zeal be according to knowledge—we, the clergy and laity of the Church of England, may yet take our place, no longer among those whose vineyard is neglected and its wall in ruins, but among those who shall "build the old waste places" and "raise up the foundations of many generations." For us there may be in store the blessing which belongs to "the repairers of the breach, and the restorers of paths to dwell in." (Isaiah lviii., 12.)

SOMERSET AND BRISTOL STEAM-PRINTING WORKS, TAUNTON.

CPSIA information can be obtained
at www.ICGtesting.com
Printed in the USA
LVHW100612210323
742065LV00002B/258

9 783382 127831